10-MINUTE PLAYS
FOR KIDS OF ALL AGES

Original short plays written for kids, to be performed by kids, for the purpose of entertaining a variety of audiences from recitals to classrooms.

Written By
Carlene Griffith

Copyright © 2016 by Carlene Griffith

All rights reserved.

Production of these plays for non-profit use is permitted. No part of this book may be reproduced. Any performance of these plays outside of non-profit use is strictly prohibited without prior authorization by the author and subject to royalties. Proof of production and production for profit purposes information can be requested by contacting GRIFFITH PLAYHOUSE at www.griffithplayhouse.com.

Acknowledgment for the said property must solely be credited to the author.

This book is dedicated to all the drama students that I've had the pleasure of teaching throughout the years.

Especially my three little drama makers at home: Nicodemus, Saphryn, and Darius.

TABLE OF CONTENTS

TRIP THROUGH TIME....................5

(7 Players, ages 5-up)

FIFTY FARTHINGS SHORT.............21

(9-12 Players, ages 5-up)

STARVING MONKEYS...................37

(11 Players, ages 5-up)

OZ'S DILEMMA........................54

(7 Players minimum, ages 8-up)

THE CASE OF THE BIG BAD WOLF......75

(16 Players, ages 8-up)

DON'T EAT THE PUDDING.............98

(10-20+ Players, ages 8-up)

THE BANK JOB......................120

(6 Players, ages 10-up)

CINDERELLA REVISITED.............139

(6 Players, ages 10-up)

ALIEN HALLOWEEN..................150

(8 Players minimum, ages 10-up)

TRIP THROUGH TIME

Having discovered time travel, Professor Ramanda, with Assistant Lenderman's help, travels through time witnessing history. Meanwhile, leaving behind a present, they don't recognize when they return.

CAST OF CHARACTERS:

PROFESSOR ROMANDA
ASSISTANT LENDERMAN
THOMAS EDISON
MELBA – Daughter of the Captain of the Pinta Ship
T-REX # 1 – dinosaur
T-REX # 2 - dinosaur
MAMA TRICERATOPS - dinosaur

SETTING:

This play begins in the present day in a scientist's laboratory. They then travel through history to the days of Thomas Edison, Columbus, and somewhere in the jungles of the Jurassic period.

LIST OF POSSIBLE PROPS:

- time machine
- cell phone
- the first light bulb
- ships wheel

- vines
- cell phone

NOTES:

Simple sets and costumes were used to show the different time periods.

When performed, I had a mix of students ages 5-18. The dialogue for the T-Rex part is simple and easy for a 5 year old. The dialogue for the Professor and Assistant parts are longer and more complicated for children 10 and up. The Dinosaurs are only meant to talk to each other. People can't understand them.

All roles, except for Thomas Edison and Mama Triceratops, can be any gender. For Melba just change the name.

SCENE 1
PROFESSOR ROMANDA'S LAB

(The scene opens in the PROFESSOR ROMANDA Lab; her ASSISTANT LENDERMAN is working on something.)

PROFESSOR ROMANDA: I did it!

ASSISTANT LENDERMAN: What did you do Professor Romanda!

PROFESSOR ROMANDA: I figured out the formula that will make the time travel machine work. I did it!

ASSISTANT LENDERMAN: That's Incredible!

PROFESSOR ROMANDA: Where shall we go?

ASSISTANT LENDERMAN: Now?

PROFESSOR ROMANDA: No better time than the present!

ASSISTANT LENDERMAN: Hmm, I don't know? There are so many choices? *(thinks a moment while holding a light bulb and looks at it)* I have always wanted to meet Thomas Edison!

PROFESSOR ROMANDA: Yes, The Wizard of Menlo Park. What a great idea!

ASSISTANT LENDERMAN: October 22, 1879, the day his invention of the light bulb worked.

PROFESSOR ROMANDA: Quick, come, let's go! Let's be witnesses to history!

(They EXIT.)

SCENE 2
WORKSHOP OF THOMAS EDISON

(THOMAS EDISON is working at a work table fiddling with a light bulb.)
THOMAS EDISON: Augh! What is wrong? Why won't this work? This should work!! *(he gets up and walks around the table thinking)*
(PROFESSOR ROMANDA and ASSISTANT LENDERMAN ENTER downstage.)
ASSISTANT LENDERMAN: Look, Professor, the sign says, "Edison Electric Light Company."
PROFESSOR ROMANDA: This is it.
PROFESSOR ROMANDA: (looking through a window) There he is! Come, let's knock.
ASSISTANT LENDERMAN: You mean to go in!
PROFESSOR ROMANDA: You said you wanted to meet him.
ASSISTANT LENDERMAN: But Professor won't that mess with history?
PROFESSOR ROMANDA: Phish... You worry too much.
(They go up to the door and knock.)
THOMAS EDISON: *(answers the door)* Yes, may I help you?
PROFESSOR ROMANDA: *(nervous)* Umm, are you Thomas Edison with the Edison Electric Light Company.
THOMAS EDISON: Yes, come in. Excuse me, I was just in the middle of an

experiment. Please wait here while I finish up a moment. I will be right with you.

(They enter and wait and watch off to the side. PROFESSOR ROMANDA'S cell phone beeps and ASSISTANT LENDERMAN gives him a "What are you doing" stare. They fiddle with it and put it away. There is a hole in PROFESSOR ROMANDA'S pocket, and the phone falls out onto the floor of the workshop. Edison completely ignores them; he is so absorbed in his work.)

THOMAS EDISON: (*fiddles with the bulb*) Okay, let us see if this will work. Awe Ha! What joy! (*dances a bit*) I've done it. Do you see... (*breathlessly*) It's the carbon filament connected to platina contact wires, that is the right combination... (*focused*) Now to see how long it will last. Shall we?

(Edison sits in amazement.)

PROFESSOR ROMANDA: That is truly amazing.

ASSISTANT LENDERMAN: We see that you are a very busy man. We will let you go and come back at a later time.

(Edison is distracted.)

THOMAS EDISON: Oh, yes, very well. Thank you for coming.

(They let themselves out and stand outside the door.)

PROFESSOR ROMANDA: That was amazing!
ASSISTANT LENDERMAN: Professor Romanda, we must be careful not to mess with the timeline or things might change for us in the future.
PROFESSOR ROMANDA: Yes, Yes, you worry too much. What could happen? Where shall we go next?
ASSISTANT LENDERMAN: hmmm. How about when Columbus came to America.
PROFESSOR ROMANDA: Yes, that would be fun. Lets go.
ASSISTANT LENDERMAN: October 12, 1492, location the Pinta ship!
(They EXIT.)
(Back in Thomas workshop, a few minutes later PROFESSOR ROMANDA'S phone beeps on the floor. Edison hears it, walks over, and picks it up.)
THOMAS EDISON: What is this curious contraption? (*studies it*) Huh, wow this is amazing! ... wait! Who were those people? Where did they go? (*EXITS off to find them*) Hello??

SCENE 3
SHIP OF THE PINTA

(MELBA EXIT)

MELBA: Yes, Papa! I will keep on the course. (*take the wheel to steer the ship*) What a beautiful day at sea, don't you think Pinta? (*talking to the ship*) What will we see today, Pinta?

(PROFESSOR ROMANDA and ASSISTANT LENDERMAN ENTER looking around. PROFESSOR ROMANDA is seasick)

MELBA: Hello there. It's a beautiful day, is it not? My father is captain of the Pinta, Martín Alonso Pinzón. He lets me steer while he naps. Don't tell Senor Columbus! Si?

(PROFESSOR ROMANDA leans over the side sick)

ASSISTANT LENDERMAN: My friend here is not feeling well.

MELBA: Here. (*she hands them a handkerchief to clean up*)

PROFESSOR ROMANDA: Thank you.

MELBA: I haven't seen either of you here before.

PROFESSOR ROMANDA: Oh, we came on board at your last stop, San Sebastián de La Gomera. I've been ill, so we've kept to ourselves.

MELBA: Yes, many have been ill. It is a long voyage. Senor Columbus is

determined to continue on until we get to Japan, so that we may trade.
ASSISTANT LENDERMAN: Yes, that is where they were supposed to be headed before they spotted the island.
MELBA: What? They? Who are you talking about?
PROFESSOR ROMANDA: Oh, my friend here is silly, confused…ignore her.
MELBA: Oh, (looks down at her compass) see here my trusty compose. It leads us on.
PROFESSOR ROMANDA: Oh, may I see it.
ASSISTANT LENDERMAN: Professor, I don't think you should…
   (MELBA hands over the compass)
PROFESSOR ROMANDA: What craftsmanship!
MELBA: Without my trusted compass, we could get lost! It is a vast ocean. I hear the Chinese are upon these waters.
ASSISTANT LENDERMAN: Professor, I think you should give the compass back. (*starts to grab for it*)
PROFESSOR ROMANDA: Wait, I'm just looking at it.
ASSISTANT LENDERMAN: Professor, Your messing with ….
PROFESSOR ROMANDA: Give it back!
(They fight over the compass, and it accidentally flies out of their hands and overboard)

MELBA: What have you done? (*shouts*) Papa!
PROFESSOR ROMANDA: Yep, time to go...
  (*ASSISTANT LENDERMAN and PROFESSOR ROMANDA scramble about and EXIT quickly*)
MELBA: My compass! (*cries*) Oh, papa?? We will be lost.
  (*EXITS off*)

SCENE 4
THE TIME MACHINE

(PROFESSOR ROMANDA and ASSISTANT LENDERMAN are back inside the time machine.)

ASSISTANT LENDERMAN: Professor Romanda, we must return home. We are messing with the timeline. Things will be changed.

PROFESSOR ROMANDA: Yes, I see you're correct. Here let me adjust the dials. *(plays with the buttons)*

ASSISTANT LENDERMAN: Professor, where is your phone?

PROFESSOR ROMANDA: What?

ASSISTANT LENDERMAN: Professor Romanda your phone? *(attempts to put her hand into PROFESSOR ROMANDA's pocket)*

PROFESSOR ROMANDA: What are you doing? Stop, *(laughing and giggling)* Stop that! *(jumps around ticklish and bumps into the machine)*

ASSISTANT LENDERMAN: Professor Romanda? The Machine? *(The machine starts)*

PROFESSOR ROMANDA: *(trying to fix it)* Wait? What? *(the machine takes off)* Hold on!

(They land and exit the machine looking around.)

ASSISTANT LENDERMAN: Where are we now Professor?

PROFESSOR ROMANDA: 200 Million years into the future… The Jurassic period!
 (They hear a loud roar.)
PROFESSOR ROMANDA: Dinosaurs!
ASSISTANT LENDERMAN: (scared) We should hide!
 (They EXIT)

SCENE 5
SOMEWHERE IN THE JUNGLE

(ENTERS two little dinosaur T-REX.)
T-REX 1: I'm so hungry.
T-REX 2: There's no food.
T-REX 1: The storm burned up everything!
T-REX 2: Mom and Dad too!
T-REX 1: My tummy is rumbling. (whines & roars)
T-REX 2: I smell something?
T-REX 1: Me too.
T-REX 2: Food! (sniffs) This way.
(The T-Rex EXIT in a hurry following their noses. A chase begins as they chase PROFESSOR ROMANDA and ASSISTANT LENDERMAN on and off stage. The T-REX having captured PROFESSOR ROMANDA and ASSISTANT LENDERMAN return dragging them back onstage wrapped in vines.)
T-REX 1: They will be tasty. One for each of us.
T-REX 2: I don't know. They look very boney.
T-REX 1: Yea, your right. Maybe we should get some herbs.
T-REX 2: Good idea. I know where some are.
(They EXIT and leave the two tied up.)

PROFESSOR ROMANDA: These Tyrannosaurus Rex are going to eat us.

ASSISTANT LENDERMAN: We should never have left our time. This is all your fault.

PROFESSOR ROMANDA: Humph!

ASSISTANT LENDERMAN: Wait, I hear something coming…

(ENTERS MAMA TRICERATOPS, who sniffs PROFESSOR ROMANDA and ASSISTANT LENDERMAN.)

ASSISTANT LENDERMAN: Awe!! It's going to eat me!!

PROFESSOR ROMANDA: This is a triceratops, silly! It's a Herbivore. It doesn't eat meat.

(MAMA TRICERATOPS goes to the corner to talk to herself. She has a moral dilemma.)

MAMA TRICERATOPS: (*roars*) Hmm, poor creatures. They're surely going to be those T-REX's meals. What should I do? Should I leave them be, or set them free? (*looks at them*) I feel bad. The storms are killing everything around here. Maybe my eggs will be safe in that box thing I found over there. (pauses) We are all going to die anyway, why should I die with guilt! I will let them go.

(She goes over to PROFESSOR ROMANDA and ASSISTANT LENDERMAN and leans in

to bite off the vine. They think she's going to bite them, so they cringe. Once they realize they're free, they run off stage. Just then, the T-REX ENTER to see their meal is gone.)

T-REX 1: Our meal!
T-REX 2: She let them free!
MAMA TRICERATOPS: You, stinky meat eaters! Yes, I set them free. What are you going to do about it?

(MAMA TRICERATOPS roars and she chases them and they all EXIT the stage.)

SCENE 6
BACK IN THE LAB

(PROFESSOR ROMANDA and ASSISTANT LENDERMAN have returned to their own time.)

ASSISTANT LENDERMAN: That was so close. We should never travel again.

PROFESSOR ROMANDA: We just need to establish some rules. There will be more trips.

(The phone rings.)

ASSISTANT LENDERMAN: Hello! … I'm sorry I don't understand you. Slow down. Sorry. I don't speak Chinese. Sorry. *(gets off the phone)* That was strange. It sounded like my mother, but she was speaking Chinese. When did my mom learn Chinese?

PROFESSOR ROMANDA: *(looking around at everything)* Everything is in Chinese!

ASSISTANT LENDERMAN: The Pinta didn't make it to America first? The Chinese must-have.

PROFESSOR ROMANDA: Look out the window. *(looks out the window)* Is that a spaceship? That car is flying!

ASSISTANT LENDERMAN: What does that say on the side of it?

PROFESSOR ROMANDA: It's in Chinese, but I think it says, "Edison's

Flying Cars!" (*they look at each other*)

(*Just then there is a roar from the other room, ASSISTANT LENDERMAN EXITS, then ENTERS again with a frantic look.*)

ASSISTANT LENDERMAN: Professor Romanda, you've got to come and see this!

(*They EXIT*)

THE END

FIFTY FARTHINGS SHORT

An orphaned young woman and her mouse friends, find themselves on the verge of losing everything if they can't come up with fifty farthings to pay the King's tax.

CAST OF CHARACTERS:
NARRATOR 1
NARRATOR 2
TAX COLLECTOR
AMANDA-RAY - lonely young woman (Cinderella-type)
MERRY - Mice 1
SHERRY - Mice 2
TERRY - Mice 3
TUFF - Mice 4
OLD MAN WATERMAN - a rich old man
LADY WATERMAN - a rich old man's wife
ESTER - the mean housekeeper
MR. MITTENS – Lady Waterman's cat

SETTING

This play takes place in a fairytale kingdom of make-believe. Set can be used within a black box theater with little or no costumes and props or an elaborate stage setting.

LIST OF POSSIBLE PROPS
- gardening tool

- scroll
- suitcase or large bag
- cane
- bag of coins
- advertisement for housekeeper

NOTES

NARRATORS, MICE and TAX COLLECTOR'S dialogue can be combined or divided if short or in need of additional players. Dialogue by other players will have to be altered to reflect changes.

In my original performance, the mice were played by students ages 5-7, and the other parts were for children ages 7-12.

Many roles are gender fluid.

SCENE 1
AMANDA-RAY'S COTTAGE

(Two NARRATORS start on stage.)
NARRATOR 1: Once upon a time in a far-off kingdom…
NARRATOR 2: Lived a lovely young lady named Amanda-ray.
NARRATOR 1: Amanda-ray lived all alone in a tiny little cottage her parents had left her when they died. It was the only thing she had.
NARRATOR 2: Her only companions in the whole world were her little Mice friends: Merry, Sherry, Terry, and Tuff.
NARRATOR 1: One day, while working in the garden, a man came to the cottage.
(The NARRATORS EXIT and the TAX COLLECTOR ENTERS.)
TAX COLLECTOR: Hello?
(AMANDA-RAY ENTERS having been working in the garden.)
AMANDA-RAY: Yes, sir, how can I help you?
TAX COLLECTOR: By order of the King, I've come to collect taxes. He asks fifty farthings.
AMANDA-RAY: Fifty, farthings! Sir, my parents have died, and all I have is this cottage. Please, sir, I have no money.

TAX COLLECTOR: Hmm, well then I will be forced to collect your cottage.
AMANDA-RAY: Sir, if you collect my home, I will have nowhere to live. What will I do?
TAX COLLECTOR: You will need to find a way and come up with 50 Farthing. I will give you one week. I'm sorry, but if you do not have the money when I come back, I will be forced to collect your home as a tax.
AMANDA-RAY: Please, sir? What will I do?
TAX COLLECTOR: I'm sorry Miss, but all I can give you is one week to figure it out.
(The TAX COLLECTOR EXITS and AMANDA-RAY EXITS the other way crying. The MICE ENTER.)
MERRY: Did you hear that?
SHERRY: Poor, Amanda-Ray!
TERRY: We have to help her.
TUFF: But what can we do?
MERRY: I have an idea! Old Man Waterman has lots of money. Maybe we can go there and find some around the house and bring it back to Amanda-Ray?
SHERRY: That's stealing!!
MERRY: Not if it's just lying around in the corners.
TUFF: I've seen money under the couch cushions.

MERRY: People who are rich drop money all the time. They won't even miss it.
TERRY: We have to do something to help Amanda-Ray!
MERRY & TERRY & TUFF: (*pleading at SHERRY*) Please???
SHERRY: Ok, but only if it's lying around!

      (*They EXIT.*)

SCENE 2
WATERMAN MANOR

(OLD MAN WATERMAN, LADY WATERMAN, ESTER, and MR. MITTENS ENTER.)

LADY WATERMAN – (*petting her cat, MR. MITTENS*) Mr. Mittens you will be good for Ester, now won't you? My sweet kitty cat! (*looks up to see WATERMAN floundering about*) Waterman! Hurry it up. It's time to go.

OLD MAN WATERMAN – (*MR. WATERMAN looking around for his glasses accidentally bumps into ESTER*) Oh, Ester! Sorry, so sorry. Could you please have my suit cleaned while we're out?

LADY WATERMAN – Dear, you're wearing your suit now.

OLD MAN WATERMAN – Oh, right, dear. Ester clean my other suit then!

ESTER – Of course, Mr. Waterman, everything will be taken care of.

LADY WATERMAN – Come, my dear, we don't want to be late.

OLD MAN WATERMAN – Yes dear, coming.

LADY WATERMAN – (*baby voice*) Bye-bye, Mr. Mittens. (*MR. MITTENS follows her to the door*)

MR. MITTENS – Meow

ESTER – Mr. Mittens. (*scoffs*) You, stinky old cat! (*she kicks at MR. MITTENS*) Get out of my way, before I

have you skinned and turned into a rug.
MR. MITTENS - Meow (*EXITS running*)
    (ESTER EXITS after him.)

SCENE 3
WATERMAN MANOR

(*NARRATOR ENTERS.*)
NARRATOR 1: Sometime later in Waterman Manor….
(NARRATOR EXITS. *MERRY ENTERS.*)
MERRY: Nobody's here, follow me.
(*SHERRY, TERRY, and TUFF ENTER.*)
SHERRY: Let's make this quick!
TERRY: I'll look under the couch.
(*The MICE scurry around looking for money.*)
TUFF: (*stops to smell something odd*) Are you sure they don't have…
(*Suddenly ENTERS MR. MITTENS, MERRY, SHERRY, and TERRY, run around while TUFF stands frozen in fear.*)
TUFF: CATS!
(*MR. MITTENS chases them around until he has them in a corner.*)
MR. MITTENS: You think that I'm going to let mice run free around my manor?? (*laughs*) You have another thing coming.
Mice: (*all beg for their lives*) Please, no Please, we'll leave! Please don't kill us! We're sorry, we'll leave.
MR. MITTENS: It's been a while since I've had "Mouse al la cart!" (*licks his lips and wrings his hands*) Yummy.

TERRY & TUFF: (*get on knees and beg*) Please, Mr. Cat sir, don't eat us.
SHERRY: I don't think we'd taste very good.
MR. MITTENS: It's Mr. Mittens, and why shouldn't I? Give me a good reason why!
MERRY: (*cowery*) Please Mr. Cat sir, I mean Mr. Mittens, we just wanted to find some money for our friend Amanda-ray, who lives down the hill. She hasn't enough money to pay the King's tax. We don't want her to lose her home.
MR. MITTENS: Oh, I see you've come to steal from us?
SHERRY: No, no, no! We were only going to pick up what was lost or left behind.
MR. MITTENS: Hmm (*pauses to think*) Okay, I won't kill you.
MERRY, SHERRY, TERRY, & TUFF: (*all the MICE breathe out a sigh of relief*)
MERRY: Thank you, oh, thank you, Mr. Cat… I mean Mr. Mittens, Sir.
MR. MITTENS: On one condition…
SHERRY: (*afraid*) What condition do you mean?
MR. MITTENS: You will help me to get rid of Ester, our Housekeeper. She is vile and a horrible person. She's got the Watermans completely fooled.
MERRY: We can do that.

MR. MITTENS: It won't be easy. You mustn't let the Watermans know you are here. If you do, they might have a reason to get rid of me, because I'm not doing my job.
SHERRY: We promise we won't.
MR. MITTENS: Then we have a deal. You get rid of my pest, and I promise not to kill you!!
MERRY, SHERRY, TERRY & TUFF: (*all together*) Deal!!!
   (The MICE EXIT one way and MR. MITTENS EXITS the other way.)

SCENE 4
WATERMAN MANOR

(*NARRATOR ENTERS*)
NARRATOR 2: The next day, Merry, Sherry, Terry, and Tuff return to Waterman Manor to fulfill the deal they had made with Mr. Mittens.
(*NARRATOR EXITS*)
ESTER: (*runs across the stage followed by MERRY & SHERRY*) EEK! Augh! Mice! Mr. Mittens!!! Get them... (*MR. MITTENS ENTERS the other direction and trots across the stage pretending to chase the mice away but instead slaps SHERRY a high five and continues off stage.*)
ESTER: (*again runs across the stage the other direction followed by TERRY & TUFF*) MR. MITTENS!!! Kill them! Catch them. Augh! EEK! (*MR. MITTENS follow again and slap TERRY a high five on the paw*)
(*OLD MAN WATERMAN & LADY WATERMAN ENTER*)
LADY WATERMAN: Ester what is all the racket down here?
ESTER: (*scampers in*) Mice! We have mice, my Lady.
OLD MAN WATERMAN: (hard of hearing) Rice, you say! We'll be having rice with dinner. Sounds good.

LADY WATERMAN: Mice? I don't see any mice. We haven't had mice here since Mr. Mittens was a kitten.

OLD MAN WATERMAN: I like rice. Brown or White?

ESTER: Mice! Not Rice. That cat hasn't caught one darn thing. There are mice chasing me around the kitchen.

OLD MAN WATERMAN: Oh, Mice, you say… Where's Mr. Mittens?

LADY WATERMAN: I don't believe a word of it! My Mr. Mittens is the best mice catcher there is.

(*MR. MITTENS ENTERS.*)

MR. MITTENS: (*rubs up to LADY WATERMAN*) Meow!

LADY WATERMAN: (*baby voice*) Mr. Mittens you wouldn't let any ugly little mice into our home, would you?

MR. MITTENS: Meow!

LADY WATERMAN: See your mistaken Ester. Get back to work and stop all your hollering.

ESTER: Yes, Ma'am. I'm sorry Ma'am.

(*LADY WATERMAN EXITS*)

Old Man WATERMAN: Oh, let me know when dinner is! I love rice. Yummy.

(*OLD MAN WATERMAN EXITS*)

ESTER: (*shakes her fist at MR. MITTENS*) You stupid CAT! Get rid of those mice, or I'll boil you in tonight's supper!

(ESTER EXITS)

NARRATOR 1: Later that night, Mr. Mittens lets Merry, Sherry, Terry, and Tuff into Ester's room. And while Ester is sleeping, Merry tickles her toes, Sherry pulls at her hair, Terry scampers around in her bed, and Tuff keeps watch for the Watermens. Ester wakes up in such a manic state that she decides she's had enough and packs up her stuff.

(ESTER ENTERS followed by OLD MAN & LADY WATERMAN.)

ESTER: Lady Waterman, I'm sorry, but I'm not going to sit around while mice are swimming around in my bed. That Cat of yours is good for nothing, and I'm sorry, but you're just going to have to find yourself another housekeeper.

LADY WATERMAN: *(throwing a temper tantrum)* Nooo, you can't leave! Who will help me with the housework? Who will cook the meals?

ESTER: That is your problem! Mr. Waterman, I'll take my last payment, please. *(puts out her hand)*

MR. WATERMAN: *(fumbles around looking for some money in his pocket)*

(MR. MITTENS trots in caring a bag of coins in his mouth.)

MR. MITTENS: Meow.

(Mr. WATERMAN looks down and grabs the coins.)

MR. WATERMAN: Oh, Thank you, Mr. Mittens. Huh… (*looks in the sack*) This should be enough.

LADY WATERMAN: Oh, (*in a baby voice*) Mr. Mittens is so smart!

ESTER: (*mad*) Oh! I hate that cat!

(ESTER grabs the money sharply and turns to storm off and EXITS.)

SCENE 5
AMANDA-RAY'S COTTAGE

(NARRATOR 2 ENTERS)

NARRATOR 2: Mr. Mittens is so grateful to the Mice for their help with getting rid of Ester, he lets them collect up as much money as they can find around the Manor. They thank him and run off as fast as they can to get the money to their dear friend Amanda-Ray.

(NARRATOR EXITS. MERRY, SHERRY, TERRY, and TUFF ENTER. They place a bag of coins on the ground with an advertisement that reads, "Help wanted for a housekeeper at Waterman Manor." AMANDA-RAY ENTERS.)

AMANDA-RAY: What's this? (*she leans down and picks up a bag and advertisement*) Oh, this is so wonderful! Oh, Merry, Sherry, Terry, and Tuff what good fortune! We won't have to leave after all.

(They all EXIT happily. NARRATORS ENTER.)

NARRATOR 1: And in the end, Amanda-Ray was able to pay the Tax Collector the fifty farthings she owed and was able to keep her cottage with Merry, Sherry, Terry, and Tuff. She also got a job as a housekeeper for Old Man and Lady Waterman.

(MR. MITTENS ENTERS)
NARRATOR 2: Mr. Mitten would agree; she is the best housekeeper they've ever had!
MR. MITTENS: Meow!

THE END

STARVING MONKEYS

When the Monkeys, who don't know they live in a zoo, go accidentally unfed for a day, they initiate a war with the Cockatoos for survival.

CAST OF CHARACTERS:
TURK - Monkey
MONA - Monkey
HOOT - Monkey
BEATRICE – Monkey
SHELIA - Cockatoo
LARRY - Cockatoo
MOE – Cockatoo
JACKIE – Cockatoo
BOB - ZooKeeper
DEBBIE – ZooKeeper
HARRY- ZooKeeper
*extra non-speaking monkey and cockatoo can be added.

SETTING:

This play takes place in the monkey habitat cage at a zoo. The cockatoos are up in the top of the trees, and the monkeys are down on the ground.

LIST OF POSSIBLE PROPS:

- fake bananas
- fake nuts

NOTES:

My students in this play were all beginners, and it was lots of fun for them to explore and develop the mannerisms of the animals with sounds and movement.

Many of the roles are gender flexible. Names can be changed.

To establish the difference between the top and bottom of the trees, I divided the stage to provide the different views. The Cockatoos looked down, and the Monkeys looked up, and they met in the middle of the stage.

SCENE 1
ZOO HABITAT

(The scene opens with two monkeys, HOOT and MONA, grooming one another.)

HOOT: I got a good one for you (takes a bug and eats it from MONA's back.)
MONA: Hum (nods yes – she never talks)
HOOT: What happens to a frog's car when it breaks down?
MONA: (raises arms and shrugs)
HOOT: It gets toad away…
MONA: (opens mouth to laugh but suddenly coughs instead)
HOOT: (over laughing) Funny huh, Mona?
  (TURK & BEATRICE ENTER, sit down, and start to look around.)
TURK: I'm hungry! (looks around)
BEATRICE: Where's the food?
MONA: (shrugs shoulders, points, and shakes head "I don't know")
HOOT: (panicking) No food? Where's the food? What?
BEATRICE: What do you mean there's no food?
TURK: Mona, hasn't the furless ape with the food come today?
MONA: (shakes head "no")
 (A nut falls from the tree above and lands on BEATRICE's head.)

BEATRICE: Ouch! (*rubs her head*)
HOOT: What is that?
TURK: (*picks up the nut*) Nut. Wait, nuts are food!
   (*They all look up.*)
TURK: Up there is food!
HOOT: That's the cockatoo's tree.
BEATRICE: That's not our food.
TURK: We need food!
MONA: (shakes his head and pats her belly.)
TURK: *(whining)* I'm hungry!
HOOT: Wait, let's look around.
BEATRICE: Maybe there's food over there.
   (*The group EXIT.*)

SCENE 2
OFFICE OF THE ZOOKEEPER AND SUPPLY STORE

ZOOKEEPER BOB: (*ENTERS talking to himself*) Ok get the monkey's food. Where did I put the monkey's food? (*yawns*) I'm so tired. I should not have stayed up so late. (*yawns again*) I need a break, just a little cat nap. The monkeys can wait. It's not like they're going to starve. I'll just take a short nap. I'll go in the back, no one will see me there. They'll just think I'm out feeding the animals. (*yawns*) Right, I'll just take a few minutes. Just a few minutes.
(*EXITS stage.*)

SCENE 3
UP IN A TREE INSIDE THE MONKEY'S HABITAT.

(SHELIA standing with her back to MOE & LARRY. She is looking around and begins complaining to both MOE and LARRY, who aren't listening.)

SHELIA: What happened here? Fruit and nuts are all over the place. You guys clean up after yourselves. I expect this tree to be presentable.
JACKIE: I tell you, Shelia, this place is totally gross.
MOE: *(not looking at her)* Uh-huh.
LARRY: *(not looking at her)* Whatever you say, Shelia.
JACKIE: Look at this mess!
SHELIA: *(realizes they're not listening)* What is wrong? You're not even listening to me.
JACKIE: What are you looking at? *(walks over to look down)* Stupid monkeys.
MOE: That one is hopping around, and that one is banging on the door.
SHELIA: Oh my! That one is hitting its head on the tree!
JACKIE: They are just stupid monkeys. They always have been.
LARRY: I've never seen them so worked up before.
SHELIA: Ignore them.
JACKIE: Yep, ignore them.

MOE: Uh, oh!
JACKIE: What now?
LARRY: They're trying to climb our tree.
SHELIA: Oh my, I do hope they aren't sick and going to spread some kind of virus.
JACKIE: Oh, dear, that would be awful. Moe, do something, will you?
MOE: What do you want me to do?
SHELIA: Fly down there and stop them.
JACKIE: Use your beak man!
LARRY: Moe, I'll take the one on the right, and you take the one on the left.
MOE: Ok, but which right? My right or your right?
LARRY: Huh? Just on the right.
MOE: Ok, (they begin to take off and bump into each other)
JACKIE: (looking down) Can't you see he's coming?
SHELIA: Stop being numbskulls and get down there at once.
LARRY: This way, not that way!
MOE: Which way?
LARRY: That way! (*they cross*)
SHELIA & JACKIE: Down! Down! Down!
MOE & LARRY: (*bump again*)
SHELIA: Oh, I can see I'll have to take the lead, follow me.
JACKIE: Let's follow her.
(They all EXIT.)

SCENE 4
BACK IN THE OFFICE OF THE ZOOKEEPER

DEBBIE: (*on the phone*) Yes, I understand. I'll head right over. (*Hangs up the phone*) Harry! There seems to be a bit of commotion over in the monkey cage. Can you go and see what's going on. (pauses and looks around) Have you seen Bob?
HARRY: Not lately. I saw him this morning over with the giraffes, but haven't seen him since.
DEBBIE: I'm going to make a few calls and see if I can find him.
HARRY: Lately, he's been taking his time getting the animals fed.
DEBBIE: It's well past feeding time.
HARRY: You might want to check supply.
DEBBIE: Ok, you head over to the monkey's habitat, and I'll check in supplies. Call me when you get there and see what the commotion is all about.
(They both EXIT.)

SCENE 5
IN THE MONKEY HABITAT

(*The MONKEYS and the COCKATOOS are engaged in battle. The MONKEYS are at the base of the tree, throwing things up at the COCKATOOS, and the COCKATOOS are dropping things on top of them to keep them from coming up the tree.*)

HOOT: I told you this was a bad idea. (*dodges a nutshell*)
MONA: (*scrambles to get the nut*)
TURK: I'm hungry.
BEATRICE: We need up that tree. (*gets pooped on the head*). Ewe, poop!
MONA: (*goes over to BEATRICE to look at the bird dropping on her head*)
TURK: Gross
HOOT: (*laughs heartedly*) How is this helping?

(*Meanwhile on the bird's side.*)

SHELIA: (*blasted him*) That's what you get dirty monkey!
JACKIE: Dirty monkey! Hahaha!
MOE: Thank goodness we had all these nutshells left over.
LARRY: They seem to be holding back.
SHELIA: Moe, you head down on the right and get the laughing one. Larry, you head down and hit the other one.

JACKIE: Ha, see what happens when you try to take over a cockatoo's nest?!
SHEILA: (*gets set to swoop down again*) I'm getting the big one in the middle. Let's go!
    (They EXIT the stage.)
HOOT: They're coming after us. Run! Quick this way.
    (They EXIT the stage.)

SCENE 6
AT THE MONKEY CAGE

HARRY: (*on the phone*) Debbie, it's Harry. Have you found Bob? No? Where is he? The monkeys and the cockatoos are having a battle over food and destroying the habitat in the process. I'm looking through the one-way window, and I don't see any sign that the monkeys got fed. Come as fast as you can with food. The feeding door is locked, so bring the key. I'll meet you at the door.
(HARRY EXITS. COCKATOOS ENTER, and They have just returned from attacking the MONKEY.)
SHELIA: Let's hold back a bit, I think they're retreating.
MOE: Good because I need a break.
JACKIE: My wing is sore from that smack attack on the big one.
LARRY: It's a good thing, we're all out of nutshells.
JACKIE: Hey isn't that Ol' Harry the Zookeeper?
SHELIA: I think his name is Harry, not Ol' Harry.
MOE: I like the girl. She's pretty.
SHELIA: You mean, Debbie.
LARRY: You know… I don't think they realize.
SHELIA: Realize? Realize what?

LARRY: The monkeys; I don't think they know that they live in a zoo.
JACKIE: Yeah, like they're still thinking they live in the jungle.
SHELIA: That's silly!
JACKIE: Look that one is trying to eat the grass.
LARRY: I haven't seen Bob today. Maybe they're hungry.
MOE: We can send them some nuts. We have plenty.
SHELIA: This is our food. Bob will be here soon enough with their food.
JACKIE: Shelia, it would be nice to share. Don't you think?
SHELIA: Then, what about us?
LARRY: We have always had plenty; we can share a little.
MOE: They can have some of my food.
SHELIA: Guys, this is stupid. Food is on the way. Look there... good Ol' Harry will get them what they need.
LARRY: They don't know that. Well, I'm going down, and I'm going to give them some nuts!
MOE: Me too.
(They EXIT.)
JACKIE: Yeah, I think I can share some too. Are you coming?
SHELIA: I guess, but only this once. Stupid monkeys
(They EXIT.)

SCENE 7
BELOW THE TREE

(The MONKEYS ENTER.)

MONA: *(slumps down on the ground crying)*

BEATRICE: It's okay

MONA: We'll figure something out.

TURK: They can't hold out forever! Winged wimps!

HOOT: I've had enough. Where is that furless ape that brings us the food every day?

BEATRICE: I've had enough of this jungle. Where I grew up, we had a banana tree in our yard. It was awesome. Every day mama would climb up and get us breakfast.

TURK: What I wouldn't do for a banana right now. I'm starving!

MONA: *(looking up, she begins to point and cowers.)*

(MOE & LARRY ENTER flying in from the side. Everybody ducks.)

HOOT: Don't peck me. We'll leave your tree alone.

MOE: Here. *(drops some nuts in front of them)*

TURK & BEATRICE: Food! *(rush to get some)*

LARRY: See, I told you they were hungry.

(JACKIE & SHELIA ENTER bringing in more nuts and some fruit.)

MONA: (*Grabs some and nods*) T h a n k Y o u
HOOT: Mona, you never talk.
BEATRICE: It's a miracle. Thank you for the food.
TURK: Thanks for not pecking at me anymore.
HOOT: But why? You were just attacking us.
LARRY: You guys don't know but the man… um, the guy that brings the food is a zookeeper.
MOE: We realized he didn't come today with your food.
JACKIE: So, yeah, we figured you must be hungry. Is that why you came up our tree?
SHELIA: We're sorry we attacked you. It wasn't very neighborly of us.
HOOT: What are you saying? The furless ape's name is Guy? He's a what? Man?
LARRY: Zookeeper. You see, we don't live in the jungle anymore, it just looks like the jungle.
BEATRICE: How do you know this?
SHELIA: Like you guys hadn't noticed you can't leave the area?
JACKIE: We can see from up high. It's a whole zoo out there of other animals.
MONA: (*freaks out a little then faints*)
LARRY: Is she going to be ok?

50

TURK, BUDDY & HOOT: (*Look at MONA then back at LARRY and shrug their shoulders.*)

TURK: I never thought about leaving? We have everything here.

HOOT: Sorry we charged your tree. We didn't know.

TURK: It was my fault. I panicked.

BEATRICE: I can't believe it! This is crazy.

> (*ENTERS HARRY & DEBBIE to the habitat holding a bag full of bananas. The MONKEYS and COCKATOOS don't speak when they enter. The animals only make monkey and bird sounds when humans are around.*)

DEBBIE: Harry careful we don't want to startle them. (slowly they pull out the bananas. *The Birds fly off EXIT as DEBBIE and HARRY come closer to the monkeys.*)

HARRY: Here, monkey, monkey! I've got a big juicy banana for you.

DEBBIE: (*Stepping over MONA*) Careful that one is sleeping.

> (*TURK and BEATRICE slowly approach the bananas. HOOT wakes up MONA. MONA sees the bananas and runs over and hugs HARRY.*)

HARRY: This is AWESOME!

DEBBIE: (nods in agreement. They pass out the rest of the food)

> (*HARRY & DEBBIE EXIT*)

HOOT: I like those furless Apes. I mean guy!
TURK: Let's save some for later.
BEATRICE: Just in case.
MONA: (*nods grabs a handful*)
(*They EXIT*)

SCENE 7
BACK IN THE ZOOKEEPER OFFICE.

(*BOB wakes up from his nap. Looks at the time and realizes he overslept.*)
BOB: Augh!! I'm so fired! (grabs a bag and EXITS)

THE END

OZ'S DILEMMA

Oz has a serious problem when he and Elpheba break up over a simple misunderstanding. She's the only one who knows his little secret, and he'll do anything to keep it that way.

The Cast of Characters:
OZ: (the wizard)
LADY ELPHEBA: (a green witch)
LADY GLINDA: (a good witch)
SARAN: (a hairstylist)
TRIBBLE: (a chef)
ASPEN: (a cat)
DORTHY: (a young girl)
*non-speaking roles can be added for extras.

SETTING:
   This play, inspired by the "Wizard of Oz," takes place in OZ's Emerald City. Scenes take place in an office, beauty salon, and apartment.

LIST OF POSSIBLE PROPS:

- witches broom
- cup for coco
- bouquet of flowers
- food tray with a bowl for soup

- nail file
- books
- 2 wands (1 for Glinda & 1 for Elpheba)
- brush or comb

NOTES:

This is a really fun play that plays around with familiar characters from the Wizard of OZ. If the kids really commit to characters, it can be very entertaining. The students that did this play were a mix from 8yrs to a teenager.

SCENE 1
OZ'S OFFICE

(We begin with OZ and ELPHEBA in OZ's office.)

OZ: It's so nice to have someone I can trust by my side.

ELPHEBA: It's so nice to have a handsome someone on my arm.

OZ: The Emerald city depends on me to be… to be… this Wizard, and I'm just a guy who floated in from Kansas.

ELPHEBA: You're a big deal to me just the way you are. Not many guys would accept me, being green and all.

OZ: (*interrupts*) Oh, yes, of course, green. (*pause*) Hey, I have an idea, maybe there's something we can mix up so that you won't be so green. What do you think?

ELPHEBA: (*shocked*) OZ, I thought it didn't bother you.

OZ: Oh, well if we're going to be a couple. You know, I am the wizard.

ELPHEBA: (*starts to get really mad*)
   (There's a knock at the door.)

OZ: Enter!

(GLINDA ENTERS.)

GLINDA: Your Honor. Elpheba. Might I have a word, Your Honor?

OZ: Certainly, Elpheba, do you mind terribly?

ELPHEBA: (*sarcastically*) I don't mind. Of course not. I don't mind that Glinda has ALL of your attention. ALL to herself. Of course not. Not at all.

OZ: Now, Elpheba, it'll just be a few moments. It's a serious city business issue.

ELPHEBA: (*shouts*) More serious than time spent with me? I see how it is! (*Grabs her broom*) Glinda, you can keep him to yourself. I'm done with him. I'll not be second place to ANYTHING, not even you Glinda!!

GLINDA: Elpheba, I think you misunderstand.

OZ: Elpheba, what are you saying?

ELPHEBA: I'm saying that it's over. You can now be free to enjoy your time with Glinda. (*to GLINDA*) The Wizard is all yours.

OZ. Elpheba?

(ELPHEBA EXITS.)

GLINDA: OZ I'm sorry. I didn't mean anything by it. I only wanted to talk to you about the color change this month.

OZ: It's ok. I'll be alright. Maybe I could just have a moment alone.

GLINDA: Yes, Your Honor. Just call if you need me. We can discuss it later.

(GLINDA EXITS.)

OZ: Oh, Elpheba! Now, this is a problem. (*paces*) She's the only one who knows I'm not a real wizard. I've got to do something. (p*aces back and forth*) I can't do it myself. She probably won't want to see me. I know! I'll mix a potion and turn her color normal. I'll have someone slip it into her drink. She'll never know. Once she realizes she's beautiful this way, she'll come back to me, and no one will know I'm not a wizard. But how?
(BLACK OUT.)

SCENE 2
EMERALD CITY BEAUTY SALON

(OZ is having his hair done by SARAN, a beautician. GLINDA ENTERS.)
GLINDA: Good morning, Your Honor. I see you're getting your hair done again.
OZ: Glinda I need your help with something, and it needs to be discreet. I have a potion that will change Elpheba's skin color from green to normal. I think the green in her skin makes her jealous without knowing it. I want her to see herself as she truly is. Can you help me?
GLINDA: Why, of course, Your Honor. What can I do?
OZ: I need someone to go in and pour the potion into her drink without her knowing it. *(pause)* Can you think of anyone who would take on such a valuable quest?
SARAN: *(steps around to face him)* I will do it for you, Your Honor. It will be easy. Elpheba has a standing appointment with me every Tuesday at 10 am. Later today, Your Honor.
OZ: That would be great. And she won't know a thing?
SARAN: I don't think so. She always has her cup of cocoa during her appointment.

GLINDA: Sounds like you have your answer. I have some business to attend to. I will be back for my appointment this afternoon, Saran. I need a new color, I think.
    (GLINDA EXITS.)
OZ: (*gets up to leave*) Great it's settled. I'll have the potion brought to you right away. (*begins to leave and turns back*) Remember to tell no one. This is the most important part. No one but us must know.
SARAN: You have my word, Your Honor. No one will know.
    (BLACK OUT.)

SCENE 3
LATER ON IN ELPHEBA'S APARTMENT

(*SARAN is working on Elpheba's hair.*)

ELPHEBA: I don't know what to do Saran. He just can't accept me for who I am. I'm green. Yes, it makes me stand out, but what else does he want me to do. I can't help that I'm green. (*crying a little*) He said green was his favorite color.

SARAN: Well, have you told him how you feel my Lady? (*hands her a tissue*)

ELPHEBA: Of course not. Why should I? I don't think it matters now anyway. I broke it off.

SARAN: Oh, that's terrible. (*grabs the cup of cocoa*) Here's your cocoa.

ELPHEBA: (*goes to drink it*) Hmmm, it smells funny.

SARAN: Oh, (*starts to get nervous*) that's weird. Are you sure? Maybe you should taste it first.

ELPHEBA: (*takes a sip and spits it out*) What is this? (*angry*) What are you trying to do to me? Are you trying to poison me?!

SARAN: (*cowering*) No, of course not my Lady. I was told it would change your color.

ELPHEBA: Change my color! How dare you! Wait, why would you? Wait. It's

not you, it's him! OZ! He's scared I'll tell….
(SARAN attempts to get up and run away.)
ELPHEBA: (*grabs SARAN by the arm*) Where are you going, Saran? I'll show him!
SARAN: I'm sorry. I'm sorry. Please have mercy on me!
ELPHEBA: Come with me. I'll show you mercy. (*laughs heartedly*)
(ELPHEBA takes SARAN and they EXIT.)

SCENE 4
OZ'S OFFICE

(OZ is sitting at his desk working when there is a knock on the door.)
OZ: Enter.
    (GLINDA ENTERS.)
GLINDA: OZ your plan backfired. She didn't drink the potion. Instead, she's turned poor Saran into a scarecrow.
OZ: She did what? *(pauses)* Did she find out it was me who asked Saran to do it?
GLINDA: I don't know? (*very upset*) All I know is I went to my appointment, and Saran's hair is now straw, and I can't get my appointment until next week. Thank you very much.
    (ENTERS TRIBBLE with a tray of food.)
TRIBBLE: Your Honor, I have your lunch as requested. (*sets it down on the table and stands to the side.*)
OZ: Thank you, Tribble. (*to GLINDA*) Now I've got to come up with a different plan? I just need to talk some sense into her. If she would just let me talk to her. (*plays with his food*)
GLINDA: (sarcastically) Your Honor, the only way you'll get her to talk

to you now is if she was asleep.
(laughs a little)
OZ: What a good idea! Tribble, do you bring Lady Elpheba her meals also?
TRIBBLE: Of course, Your Honor. She trusts no one but me to make her special pea soup.
OZ: Tribble, I have a special request for you. But you must keep it a secret.
TRIBBLE: You have my complete devotion, Your Honor. What would you like me to do?
GLINDA: *(crosses to the door)* I'm leaving before I get myself into trouble with her. The less I know, the better.
(GLINDA EXITS.)
OZ: Tribble, I need you to get some poppies and hide them in a bouquet that you deliver to Lady Elpheba.
TRIBBLE: But Your Honor, won't that make her fall asleep?
OZ: That is the point. That way, I can talk to her.
TRIBBLE: But how do I not fall asleep bringing it to her?
OZ: I'll give you an antidote that will keep you from falling asleep. I use it all the time. Come with me, and I'll get it for you.
(OZ & TRIBBLE EXIT.)

SCENE 5
ELPHEBA'S APARTMENT

(ELPEPHA is sitting reading at a table waiting for her meal. There is a knock, and TRIBBLE ENTERS with a food tray and a bouquet of flowers.)
ELPHEBA: What do we have today, Tribble?
TRIBBLE: It's my Lady's favorite, pea soup.
ELPHEBA Oh, Tribble you're the only one who makes it the way I like it.
TRIBBLE: Here you are, my Lady. (*sets the flowers down on the table*) You have a secret admirer.
ELPHEBA: Oh, I'm sure it's no secret. He's at it again, isn't he? Wait, why do I feel so sleepy. (*Yawns*) What is… Poppies! (*gets up from her seat*) Tribble, you brought me poppies! Throws them down on the ground. OZ put you up to this too didn't he? Well, I'll show him.
TRIBBLE: I didn't mean to my Lady. He said he just wanted to talk to you.
ELPHEBA: Talk to me, or drug me? (*pause*) He's trying to get rid of me because I know his little secret. Well, it won't be long until we all know his secret. Until then, you! (*grabs TRIBBLE by the arm*)

65

TRIBBLE: Please, my Lady, I was only doing what he asked me.
ELPHEBA: Take me to your kitchen. I have a surprise for him (*laughs heartedly*)
    (TRIBBLE & ELPHEBA EXIT.)

SCENE 6
BACK IN OZ'S OFFICE.

(OZ is at his table when GLINDA storms in.)

GLINDA: You've done it again. She's turned poor Tribble's skin to tin! Tribble doesn't even remember his own name.

OZ: Dang it! I thought for sure it would work this time. *(pause)* This time I'll make her come to me. Send for Aspen!

GLINDA: Not your pet cat.

OZ: Yes, bring my darling Aspen.

GLINDA: I'll have nothing to do with it.

OZ: Elpheba has always loved Aspen, my cat.

(GLINDA & OZ EXIT.)

SCENE 7
ELPHEBA'S APARTMENT

(ELPHEBA is doing her nails when there's a knock at the door. She goes to the door and finds ASPEN the cat.)

ELPHEBA: (*gives Aspen a little pet*) Aspen! What are you doing here?

ASPEN: Meow!

ELPHEBA: Come in! I knew he wouldn't give up, but he's low to think he can get me back with you.

ASPEN: (*purrs and rubs herself against ELPHEBA's legs.*)

ELPHEBA: (w*aves her wand to make ASPEN speak*) I give you speech. Tell me, Aspen, what is going with OZ?

ASPEN: (*coughs a little and clears her throat*) Wow, I can speak. Thank you, Elpheba. I've always loved your ability to use magic.

ELPHEBA: What is going on in the palace?

ASPEN: We'll, of course, I don't approve, but OZ is trying to find ways to get you to come back to him. He sent me to you in hopes that you would forgive him.

ELPHEBA: Has he given up this notion that I'm going to change my color for him?

ASPEN: That I don't know. You should ask Glinda.

68

ELPHEBA: *(paces back and forth with her wand in hand)* Glinda! Glinda! OOOH, I do hate that witch. She thinks she's so much better than me. Just because she's not green.

ASPEN: Well if only everyone had fur like mine, then there would be no problem.

ELPHEBA: What do you know, you're just a cat.

ASPEN: *(snobby)* OZ's cat if you don't mind.

ELPHEBA: Oh, is that right? *OZ's* cat. How about OZ's lion? I'm going to give you an upgrade Aspen.

ASPEN: Oh, I'm not sure I like where this is going.

ELPHEBA: Oh, don't be such a scaredy-cat. I think you're going to like being a lion.

ASPEN: Lion!!! Oh, I don't think so. *(runs out)*

(ASPEN EXITS.)

ELPHEBA: *(running after Aspen)* Get back here you scaredy-cat! I'll get you, Oh, I will get you. *(She runs after the cat)*

(ELPHEBA EXITS.)

SCENE 8
BACK IN OZ'S OFFICE

(OZ runs in and slams the door behind him. Panting and blowing as though he's been scared to death. After a few minutes, he begins to sit down when there's a knock at the door.)

OZ: *(startled and scared he puts his face against the door to listen)* Who is it?

GLINDA: *(from the other side of the door)* Your honor, it's Glinda!

OZ: Is there a lion with you?

GLINDA: No! It's gone. Can I come in?

OZ: *(opens the door slowly)* Okay. *(looks around, then shuts and locks the door)* Where did it go?

GLINDA: You mean, Aspen, your cat, who is now a LION!!! *(she's angry)*

OZ: That was Aspen?!?

GLINDA: She ran off into the forest after I shot off some sparks from my wand. You won't need to worry about her, I think.

OZ: *(shakes his head)* Aspen! My poor little cat. What has Elpheba done? *(sits down with this head down between his hands then looks up at GLINDA)* Why would she do that? *(stands up)* She tried to have Aspen KILL me! My own cat.

GLINDA: Your Honor you have to go to her yourself.
OZ: Why so she can turn me into a frog? *(sits down)*
GLINDA: If you love her, go to her!
OZ: (*shoots up from his seat*) I don't love her.
GLINDA: Oh, I thought you were doing this to get her back?
OZ: I… well, (*paces*) I don't want… *(stops pacing)* Never mind. You wouldn't understand. *(paces again)* Things are getting desperate. She can't keep hurting people. (*stops pacing*) She must be stopped. (*speaking to himself*) We have to get her broom.
GLINDA: Why her broom?
OZ: She stores her wand in it. Without her wand, she can't hurt anyone. (*looking at GLINDA*) Who can get her wand?
GLINDA: (*getting angry*) OZ there are more important things right now that must be discussed. Elpheba's sister, Lady Eveline of the East, has been killed!
OZ: How?
GLINDA: A house has been dropped on her.
OZ: What? (*seats down*) I thought Elpheba loved Eveline? (*confused*) She would never.

71

GLINDA: No, this is a young witch by the name of Dorothy. She's on her way here now. She wants you to get her home. Can you help her?
OZ: Help her? … Why …? Why, of course, I can! (*stands up*) I'm the Wizard! The Wizard of OZ can do anything.
GLINDA: That's what I thought. You are such a wonderful Wizard, your Honor.
OZ: Wonderful. I need to prepare for her arrival.
GLINDA: Of course, Your Honor.
(GLINDA EXIT.)
OZ: (*Goes and sits down at his desk*) Oh, I wish it didn't have to come to this!
(BLACK OUT.)

SCENE 9
LATER THAT EVENING IN OZ'S OFFICE.

(OZ sits at his desk. There is a knock on the door.)

OZ: Enter!

(DOROTHY ENTERS.)

DOROTHY: Your Honor. (*curtseys*) Your Wizard-ness!

OZ: Do you know who I am?

DOROTHY: I was told you were the Wizard.

OZ: Yes, you're correct. Who are you?

DOROTHY: My name is Dorothy Gale from Kansas.

OZ: What can I do for you?

DOROTHY: I want to go home, back to Kansas.

OZ: Kansas, you say! Well, I can get you back to Kansas, but you must do something for me first.

DOROTHY: Anything Your Honor. Also, I have three friends who also have come with me. They would like your help too.

OZ: Three friends, you say.

DOROTHY: Yes, they're waiting outside. They said only I could come in and see you.

OZ: Who are these friends of yours? Are they from Kansas too?

DOROTHY: No, my friends are the Scarecrow, the Tin Man, and the

Cowardly Lion. They live here in OZ. They …
OZ: (*interrupts*) Oh, I see. Hmm...If you and your friends want my help, you must get Elpheba's broom. (*to self*) That wicked witch.
DOROTHY: Oh, but how am I supposed to get a wicked witch's broom from her.
OZ: You killed Eveline! You'll find the way.
DOROTHY: That was an accident!
OZ: If you don't get me that broom, I'll make sure you never see Kansas again!
DOROTHY: OH!
THE END

THE CASE OF THE BIG BAD WOLF

Granny Hood is missing, and everyone is pointing the finger at the Big Bad Wolf. With a line of storybook witnesses testifying against him, only the White Rabbit can prove his innocence. If not, it's off with his head!

CAST OF CHARACTERS:
BIG BAD WOLF (aka Wolfie)
RED RIDING HOOD
GRANNY HOOD
WOODSMAN - Bailiff
LITTLE PIGGY 1
LITTLE PIGGY 2
LITTLE PIGGY 3
QUEEN OF HEARTS - Judge
WHITE RABBIT- Attorney for the Defense
MAD HATTER - Attorney for the Prosecution
PINOCCHIO - Surprise witness
HUMPTY DUMPTY - Jury 1
JACK - Jury 2
Little BO PEEP - Jury 3
MARY - Jury 4
SLEEPING BEAUTY -Jury 5
*Other non-speaking characters can be added if needed.

SETTING:
This whole play takes place in a fairy tale land courtroom.

LIST OF POSSIBLE PROPS:
- red Mallet
- tea cup
- fake lamb

NOTES:
The Little Piggys are referred to as sisters but can be any gender. The dialogue will need to be changed to reflect the difference.

This is a very silly play. The more committed the players are to their characters, the more successful the performance will be.

Sound effects are also an important part of this play.

SCENE 1
COURTROOM FOR FAIRYTALE CREATURES

WOODSMAN: All please stand for Her Honor the Queen of Hearts
(All stand as QUEEN OF HEARTS ENTERS.)
QUEEN OF HEARTS: You may all be seated. But just know I'm watching you. Any funny business and it's off with your heads. Woodsmen begin! (s*lams down her mallet*)
WOODSMAN: (*reading from a scroll*) Your Honor, today we're here regarding case #2009 "Make-believe creatures versus the Big Bad Wolf." We have the Mad Hatter to represents the prosecution and White Rabbit…. (*looks around*) for the defense.
QUEEN OF HEARTS: White Rabbit? Where is that rabbit?
MAD HATTER: Tea anyone?
(Everyone looks around for WHITE RABBIT. WHITE RABBIT is at the back of the auditorium and rushes in from the back of the audience muttering to himself the whole way to the stage, "I'm late, excuse me, no time for you, I'm late I'm late I'm late!")
WHITE RABBIT: (*once on stage he rushes in breathing heavily*) I'm here, your honor. I'm late, oh, I'm late for this very important date.

QUEEN OF HEARTS: Don't let it happen again! (*slams down her mallet*)
WHITE RABBIT: Yes, Your Honor. I'm very sorry. Sorry, Your Honor. So sorry.
QUEEN OF HEARTS: Get on with it! Mad Hatter, what is your accusation?
MAD HATTER: Crimes of terror, violence, and ravenous hunger against the little, "oh so sweet" innocent fairy tale creatures of this here make-believe kingdom. We the people accuse him (*pointing to WOLFIE*) of the attempted murder of Little Piggy 1, 2, and 3, Little Red Riding Hood, and Granny Hood who is still missing.
QUEEN OF HEARTS: White Rabbit how does the defendant plea?
WHITE RABBIT: Not guilty Your Honor.
   (*Everyone in the courthouse "awe" and "oh" at one another*)
QUEEN OF HEARTS: Well, looks like we're going to have a little fun here. And then it's OFF WITH HIS HEAD! Begin.
MAD HATTER: (*to the jury*) I will attempt to prove here today...(*distracted*) tea anyone?
LITTLE RED RIDING HOOD: That comes later.
MAD HATTER: What?

LITTLE RED RIDING HOOD: Mr. Hatter, if you don't mind, please finish your sentence.
MAD HATTER: Oh, where was I?
LITTLE RED RIDING HOOD: today...
MAD HATTER: Today?
LITTLE RED RIDING HOOD: You said, I will attempt to prove here today...
MAD HATTER: What will you prove?
LITTLE RED RIDING HOOD: No you said you'd prove here today...
MAD HATTER: I said I'd prove... I'd prove something. Oh my, that's quite silly now, isn't it? A little mad, you might say.
LITTLE PIGGY 3: Get it together, man!
LITTLE PIGGY 1: Must you be so bossy.
LITTLE PIGGY 2: Mr. Hatter, please finish your statement.
MAD HATTER: I really just don't know where I am...
LITTLE RED RIDING HOOD: The Big Bad Wolf tried to eat us? Remember?
MAD HATTER: Oh, yes, that's right. I'm here to prove that he tried to eat them all for lunch.
(*Everyone reacts with "Oh" and "awe" and "that's awful!" etc.*)
QUEEN OF HEARTS: Thank you for that. (*looking at the Jury*) Shall we cut off his head?
(*The jury all nod in agreement.*)

WHITE RABBIT: Your Honor! I've not been able to present my case yet. I will prove my client's innocence. My client has the misfortune of being pre-judged based on the fact that he is a wolf. But I'm here to tell you that you are very much misguided. Not all wolves have a vicious hunger. I will present the facts for what they are and not assumed.
QUEEN OF HEARTS: All right, I guess if we have to, let's hear a testimony.
MAD HATTER: Ooh, ooh, I have a witness. Pick me, pick me!
QUEEN OF HEARTS: Okay, Mad Hatter, call your first witness.
MAD HATTER: I call the Three Little Pigs.
WOODSMAN: Three Little Pigs, please take the stand.

(All three little pigs take the stand to testify.)

MAD HATTER: Little Piggy 1, 2, and 3, can you please tell the court what occurred to you on a fortnight?
LITTLE PIGGY 1: I'll go first since I was the one to first encounter the Big Bad Wolf.
LITTLE PIGGY 2: Why does she always go first? Not fair.
LITTLE PIGGY 3: Give me a break. Let the pig tell her story.
LITTLE PIGGY 1: You can go next.

LITTLE PIGGY 2: (crosses arms in protest)

LITTLE PIGGY 1: Well, there I was, minding my own business, gardening flowers, at my sweet little house made of straw, when I heard something blow like a horn in the forest. Then I saw his piercing eyes staring at me through the bush. Frightened, I ran into the house. I could hear him calling after me. "Oh Little Piggy, excuse me, Little Piggy!" But I got inside before it was too late. I could hear him puffing and blowing, and before I knew it (*starting to cry*), my sweet little house of straw was in pieces all around me. Terrified, I ran as fast as my little legs could take me to my sister's house made of sticks. I thought I'd be safe there.

(SLEEPING BEAUTY interrupts with a rather large snore that wakes her up. Everyone looks over at her sitting in the jury's section.)

SLEEPING BEAUTY: (*sheepishly*) Excuse me.

LITTLE PIGGY 2: It's my turn.

LITTLE PIGGY 3: I told you straw was too soft and would never last through anything.

LITTLE PIGGY 1: Fine! (*to LITTLE PIGGY 2*) It's your turn. (*to LITTLE PIGGY 3*) Know it all!

LITTLE PIGGY 2: I'm at home working on a puzzle in my nice little house made of sticks when I hear a pounding at the door. It's my sister whom I let in of course. And before she can tell me what the matter is, I hear a dark grizzly voice outside my door. "Let me in, let me in or I'll" ….and before he could finish, he blew, and he blew my house right down around us. Terrified, we ran as fast as we could to our sister's house made of brick. The Wolf followed. I mean he was on the warpath or something. He was right behind us. I could hear him growling something out as we ran away but who could understand him through those ferocious teeth.

LITTLE PIGGY 3: All right, you've said enough. Let me take a turn.

LITTLE PIGGY 2: Excuse me.

LITTLE PIGGY 3: Yeah, so there I was making my favorite soup when out of the window I hear these two crying and screaming their lungs out. I told them both that straw and sticks alone would never last the likes of any storm. Especially a Big Bad Wolf. You see, back in 2000, we had ourselves a wallop of a storm. You'd have thought these little piggies would've learned their lesson then, but "Oh No" they wouldn't listen to

me. They just went on and on about the economy and how it was unaffordable and going green. I mean really, you got to invest in what matters. Safety matters. That's my motto. I say your safety is worth the price.
LITTLE PIGGY 1: Are you going to get to the point?
LITTLE PIGGY 3: Oh, fine. So they came in screaming and slammed the door. I knew that there was nothing that Wolf could do to knock down my house. Best brick in this here county.
LITTLE PIGGY 2: (*clears her throat*)
LITTLE PIGGY 3: So we hear him outside, huffing and blowing, pleading to let him in. But no way Jose! He's not getting in my den. So then we hear him up on the roof. Thank goodness, I was making my pot of soup. That darn Wolf fell right down my chimney into the pot. Burned his fur right off. He jumped so high that he landed right outside the door. I told you no one was getting into my den. I showed him who's boss. We watched him run away down the lane. We hadn't heard a thing from him since until we heard about poor old Granny and Little Red. Not a bone or hair of her head was found. It's a shame, that darn ol'

Wolf. I bet you her cabin was made of logs. You can't trust them logs. I tell you, brick that's the only way to go.
(We hear a large crash as HUMPTY DUMPTY falls off his chair)
QUEEN OF HEARTS: What was that?
JACK: Quick, someone call for the king's horses and the king's men, Humpty has fallen off his chair again!
(Everyone stands up to get a better look as WOODSMAN rushes over)
WOODSMAN: No need, I've got him. (*helping HUMPTY DUMPTY up*)
HUMPTY DUMPTY: I'm all right. Sorry about that. I just slipped. I'll be all right.
QUEEN OF HEARTS: Order! Order! Let's get on with this! (*slams down her mallet*)
WHITE RABBIT: I'd like to cross-examine the witnesses, Your Honor.
QUEEN OF HEARTS: Go ahead.
WHITE RABBIT: Piggys, did anyone of you actually talk to the wolf as he approached you?
LITTLE PIGGY 1, 2, and 3: (*looking at each other*) No!
WHITE RABBIT: How do you know that he didn't just want to talk to you or ask you a question and be on his way?

LITTLE PIGGY 1: Well, he had such piercing big eyes.
LITTLE PIGGY 2: And he had such a deep growling voice.
LITTLE PIGGY 3: And such ferocious teeth.
WHITE RABBIT: So none of you took the time to get to know him because of the way he looked.
LITTLE PIGGY 1,2, and 3: Yes.
WHITE RABBIT: Did the Big Bad Wolf hurt any of you?
LITTLE PIGGY1: No
LITTLE PIGGY 2: But he blew down our houses.
WHITE RABBIT: Could that have been an accident?
LITTLE PIGGY 3: A tornado is an accident. This guy tried to eat us.
WHITE RABBIT: Did he ever say he was going to eat you?
LITTLE PIGGY 1, 2, and 3: No
WHITE RABBIT: Thank you. That will be all. Your Honor I would like to call my first witness.
QUEEN OF HEARTS: Very well.
WHITE RABBIT: I would like to call Pinocchio to the stand.
MAD HATTER: I object. This witness wasn't even in these stories.
QUEEN OF HEARTS: What is this witness's relevance to these stories?

WHITE RABBIT: He was there at the scene of the crime.
QUEEN OF HEARTS: Proceed.
(PINOCCHIO takes the stand.)
WHITE RABBIT: Pinocchio where do you reside?
PINOCCHIO: Currently, I live at my father Gepetto's wood carving shop.
WHITE RABBIT: And where did you live before that?
PINOCCHIO: In the trunk of a tree, in the Hundred Acre Wood.
WHITE RABBIT: And where is that in proximity to Granny's house?
PINOCCHIO: At a fork in the road, down Dowry Lane and the path to Granny's house.
WHITE RABBIT: Can you tell me what you saw a fortnight?
PINOCCHIO: I saw Little Red Riding Hood come to the fork and approach the Big Bad Wolf who lives in the bush there.
WHITE RABBIT: She approached him. Then what?
PINOCCHIO: Then she smiled and gave him a cookie and took off down Dowry Lane.
WHITE RABBIT: Thank you. Mr. Hatter, your witness.
MAD HATTER: You say you saw Little Red Riding Hood talk to the Big Bad Wolf.
PINOCCHIO: Yes.

MAD HATTER: And what did they say to one another?
PINOCCHIO: (stutters) Um, well, I'm sure she said something like, "Where can I find some fresh flowers?" And he said something like "down this path."
MAD HATTER: Whatever do you mean? Did they say this or not?
PINOCCHIO: Uh, huh!
  (PINOCCHIO's nose begins to grow, and everyone reacts noisily.)
MAD HATTER: Your nose is growing! Are you telling the truth?
PINOCCHIO: Um, well…
  (PINOCCHIO's nose grows longer.)
MAD HATTER: Did they really say these things?
PINOCCHIO: (*beginning to cry*) I don't know! I only saw them. The woodcarver hadn't carved my ears yet. I couldn't hear what they said; I only saw them.
MAD HATTER: Your honor I'm finished with this witness.
  (PINOCCHIO runs from the courtroom crying and then suddenly we hear a load "baa" from MARY's little Lamb.)
MARY: (*calling*) Lamby! Here Lamby! (*to the Queen*) Sorry, Your Honor, she follows me wherever I go?
BO PEEP: Hey, that's my lamb! I'd thought I lost my sheep.

MARY: Oh, how do you know that's not my lamb? Is your lamb's fleece white as snow?
BO PEEP: You stole my sheep.
MARY: Did not.
BO PEEP: Did so?
QUEEN OF HEARTS: Order! Order! Or I'll cut off your heads. (*it gets very quiet*) Woodsman, please take the sheep out of the courtroom. Can we please continue?
MAD HATTER: Your Honor, my next witness is Little Red Riding Hood.
WOODSMAN: Little Red Riding Hood will you please take the stand.
   (LITTLE RED RIDING HOOD takes the stand.)
MAD HATTER: Will you tell the court what happened to you the other night?
LITTLE RED RIDING HOOD: I was asked by my mother to go to Granny's house and bring her some goodies because she was sick and not feeling well. So on my way, I ran into the Big Bad Wolf. I was scared at first because my mother told me not to talk to any strangers and go straight there. But he seemed nice enough. He asked me where I was going, and I told him I was going to Granny's house. He convinced me that she would appreciate some flowers and that I could find the prettiest ones down

Dowry Lane. So I thought that would be nice and went after the flowers. Once I had enough flowers for a bouquet, I headed over to Granny's house. When I got there, the door was unlocked, and the lights were out. I called out to her, and I heard this deep, growling voice respond. "Yes, my dear!" I saw these enormous eyes and huge teeth. And then the wolf said, "What better to eat you with my dear!" I screamed, and just then the Woodsman appeared at the door with an ax. The wolf jumped from the bed and was wearing Granny's clothes. Granny was nowhere to be found. I can't remember what happened after that. I think I passed out from fear.

MAD HATTER: Thank you, Red. White Rabbit, your witness.

WHITE RABBIT: You say the Big Bad Wolf asked you first where you were going?

LITTLE RED RIDING HOOD: Yes.

WHITE RABBIT: You also say he seemed nice enough.

LITTLE RED RIDING HOOD: Well he did at the time.

WHITE RABBIT: And you've testified that your mother asked you not to talk to strangers and go right to your Granny's house. But instead, you talked to the wolf and then

picked flowers first. Clearly, you do not always do what you're supposed to.
MAD HATTER: I Object.
QUEEN OF HEARTS: Sustained.
WHITE RABBIT: What was it that the Big Bad Wolf said to you in response to your observation of his big eyes and big teeth?
LITTLE RED RIDING HOOD: He said: "the better to eat you with my dear!"
WHITE RABBIT: "the better to eat YOU with my dear!" or "the better to eat with my dear?"
LITTLE RED RIDING HOOD: I'm not sure. I was really scared. It was so dark, and everything was so weird.
WHITE RABBIT: Did the Wolf jump out of bed before the Woodsman appeared at the door or after?
LITTLE RED RIDING HOOD: As I said, I'm not sure, I kind of started to go black at that moment.
WHITE RABBIT: So you're not really sure which way it went, are you?
LITTLE RED RIDING HOOD: Well, I don't know it was all crazy for a bit there.
WHITE RABBIT: That's enough. Thank you. Your Honor I'd like to call the Big Bad Wolf up to the stand.
QUEEN OF HEARTS: Finally, we're getting to the good part.

(Suddenly there's a huge crashing sound outside the courthouse, everyone pears out into the audience, as though they're looking out the window.)

SLEEPING BEAUTY: Is that a Bean Stock?

JACK: Uh, oh! My beans! (searches pockets) I lost my beans.

BO PEEP: What's that?

MARY: It looks like a Giant.

BO PEEP: My lamb!

MARY: Your lamb, that's my lamb.

SLEEPING BEAUTY: Not anymore. The Giant has just eaten your lamb.

JACK: Oops. Sorry girls.

BO PEEP & MARY: (crying) JACK!

HUMPTY DUMPTY: Poor thing, if only the king's horses and king's men could put Lamby back together again.

BO PEEP & MARY: (start to cry louder)

QUEEN OF HEARTS: Order! Order! Or it's off with your heads.

(Everyone goes back to their seats.)

WOODSMAN: Big Bad Wolf will you please take the stand.

(BIG BAD WOLF takes the stand.)

WHITE RABBIT: Please state your name for the record.

BIG BAD WOLF: Big Bad Wolf

WHITE RABBIT: Is that the name you go by?

BIG BAD WOLF: No, I like to go by Wolfie. I was named after my father. Unfortunately, he was just Wolf until he got into trouble. That's where the Big Bad part came from. I'm not like my father. I'm a vegetarian. I don't eat meat. I'm allergic to it. That's why I think this is all so absurd. If I had eaten anyone or had wanted to, I would blow up like a blowfish.

WHITE RABBIT: Can you tell us what happened on a fortnight when you had your encounter with the Three Little Pigs.

BIG BAD WOLF: You bet I can. I had this terrible cold. I think it was the swine flu. I was feeling so terrible, sneezing and coughing. My nose was running something awful. I knew that the three little pigs lived nearby, so I thought I'd go ask them what I could do to get better, being that they're swine and all. But the minute I get there, that Little Piggy starts hollering and runs off before I can even talk to her. Unfortunately, I sneezed so hard that I blew her house down. I didn't know that you could build a house out of straw?

WHITE RABBIT: So you're saying it was an accident?

BIG BAD WOLF: Yes, and I felt terrible about it. I tried to follow her and apologize and ask her what I could do? But when I got to the other piggy's house, no one would let me in. Then the sneezing started again, and I couldn't stop it. So I blew the second house down. Oh, boy did this make me feel even worse. I saw them go to the other Piggy's house made of brick and thought maybe if I could just talk to them, they would listen. All I wanted was some help with my flu and to apologize for their houses. I knew they wouldn't listen. Everyone always runs when they see me. I can't help it that I look like this. It was hard to talk with my throat hurting as it did. I sounded so grizzly. So I thought if I could just get them to listen. I climbed up the roof and was going to yell down the chimney when I sneezed again and lost my grip and fell down the chimney. I landed in the pot and burned my fur right off. I knew then that I just had to get away before they killed me. I ran for my life. I decided it was best to just stay in my bush and wait out the flu.

WHITE RABBIT: Can you tell us what happened later?

BIG BAD WOLF: Little Red Riding Hood came by and asked me where she could find the prettiest flowers for her Granny's bouquet. I love Granny. She always gives me a good scratch and fills my belly with the best goodies. I would never hurt Granny. After Little Red Riding Hood told me about Granny being sick and all, I thought maybe she'd know what to give me to help me feel better. When I got to Granny's house, I noticed that she wasn't there. I decided to wait for her. She's always so kind to me.

WHITE RABBIT: Why were you in Granny's bed?

BIG BAD WOLF: I had chills, so I grabbed her nightgown and jumped into her bed to rest a bit until she got back. But Red came in first and started asking about my eyes and teeth. I've got big teeth. See!

WHITE RABBIT: Did you tell Little Riding Hood that you were going to eat her?

BIG BAD WOLF: I never said: "the better to eat you with!" I said, "the better to eat with" I mean big teeth, big bites.

WHITE RABBIT: Do you know where Granny is?

BIG BAD WOLF: I don't know where Granny is. With her being sick, and all, I sure am worried. She's the best lady.
WHITE RABBIT: Did you attack the Woodman?
BIG BAD WOLF: No! He scared the life out of me with that ax, waving it all around. I was grateful to get out of there alive.
WHITE RABBIT: What happened after you left?
BIG BAD WOLF: I went back to my bush. Sick, furless, and cut by an ax. I'm the victim here. Discrimination is what this is all about. I didn't eat anyone. Just because I'm a wolf doesn't make me the bad guy. Sure my name is Big Bad Wolf, but as I said, that's my dad. Not me.
(Suddenly there's another big bang outside.)
QUEEN OF HEARTS: What is it this time?
(GRANNY ENTERS.)
LITTLE RED RIDING HOOD: Granny! Oh, Granny, we thought you were dead. We thought the Big Bad Wolf had eaten you. Where have you been?
BIG BAD WOLF: Granny, are you ok? We've been so worried about you. What happened to you?

GRANNY: Your Yonor! Please, there has been a huge misunderstanding. Wolfie would never eat me. He's perfectly harmless. Wolfie is my friend and a vegetarian. He would never eat meat, especially swine meat.
LITTLE PIGGY 1: Well, I never
LITTLE PIGGY 2: Thank goodness for that.
LITTLE PIGGY 3: You keep telling yourself that Grandma.
LITTLE RED RIDING HOOD: Where have you been? We've been looking for you.
GRANNY: Well, I've been sick with the swine flu and just feeling terrible. I'm sorry, Wolfie. I think I passed it on to you. I decided to go to the Palace and see Snow White's Stepmother. I hear she's got a few good concoctions up her sleeve. She got me a potion that truly knocked my feet out from under me. I got home and brewed it up and took some. And as I went to get my warm hood from the closet, I became sleepy, slipped, and fell into a pile of yarn on the floor. Feels like I was asleep for an eternity. I've been there, in the closet all tied up this whole time. Once I woke up, I got out of there and come straightway to look for Wolfie and

tell him about the potion. I feel a hundred percent better. Thank goodness I ran into Pinocchio, or I would've never known about all this nonsense. Your Honor, please don't cut off his head.
QUEEN OF HEARTS: Don't cut off his head! Order! Order! (*slams down her mallet*) What's this? What's this? Someone has painted my mallet red! Who has painted my mallet red? Off with his head, whoever has painted my mallet red!!!!
WOODSMAN: (*runs off stage*) Run for your life!
　　(*Everyone screams and runs off stage.*)

THE END

DON'T EAT THE PUDDING

It's up to Billy and his Grandfather to stop aliens, who have taken over the senior home, from abducting the unsuspecting residents.

CAST OF CHARACTERS:
MOM
DAD
GRANDPA
BILLY
BETTY
HONEY BEE LEADER
HONEY BEE #2
HONEY BEE #3
HONEY BEE #4
EXTRA HONEY BEES
CAPTAIN
ALIEN STAFFER #2
ALIEN STAFFER #3
ALIEN STAFFER #4
EXTRA ALIEN STAFFERS
EUGENE
SENIORS CITIZEN #2
SENIORS CITIZEN #3
SENIORS CITIZEN #4
*EXTRA SENIORS CITIZENS

SETTING:
This is a modern-day play that takes place in a senior living home. The whole play is done in one room.

LIST OF POSSIBLE PROPS:
- trays
- pudding cups & spoons
- newspapers
- couch cushions
- radio/stereo

NOTES:
Singing is important for the plot of this play. There are a few music cues. Songs can be sung with or without any music. Any campy song or original song should work.

The play takes place all in one room so blackouts can be used at the end of a scene. They are not indicated in the script, because we did not use them in our performance. Only dimming of lights was used to indicate a change in the day to night.

SCENE 1
SENIOR COMMON ROOM

(We open to a room full of SENIORS CITIZENS sitting around in comfy chairs chatting while STAFFERS are walking around tending to them.)

EUGENE: When do we get that pudding?

SENIORS: *(all together)* Yay, pudding! Get me pudding!

(SENIORS start to make a fuss)

CAPTAIN: After visiting hours.

EUGENE: *(anxious)* I want some NOW! *(tries to stand up & falls back down)*

STAFFER #2: Hold your horses, Eugene! *(Rushes over to help)*

CAPTAIN: *(very commanding)* I said after visiting hours.

STAFFER #3: *(to CAPTAIN)* Maybe we should just give it to them now, Sir?

CAPTAIN: You don't think it would be a little odd if visitors came and found all of their loved ones unconscious mid-day?

STAFFER#3: You have a point, Sir.

CAPTAIN: There is a reason the Order made me Captain and *you* a Nurse. I do the thinking, and you do the following.

STAFFER#3: Yes, Sir. Captain Sir. *(returns to tending seniors)*

CAPTAIN: *(mumbles/sighs)* minions…

SENIORS CITIZEN #2: Why can't we listen to the radio?
STAFFER #2: Enjoy the quiet. It's so peaceful.
STAFFER #4: You folks are mighty feisty tonight. Calm Down!
STAFFER #2: *(hushed to STAFFER 3)* Maybe we should give that one some EXTRA Pudding tonight?
CAPTAIN: *(to STAFFER 3 & 4)* Report to the kitchen and prep the Glook for the Pudding. We'll make it EXTRA strong tonight. Tomorrow is a full moon. I don't want any of the new recruits to slow down the process. We only have one night. The ship will arrive promptly at midnight. The Order demands perfection!
   (STAFFERS 3 & 4 EXIT.)

SCENE 2
SENIOR COMMON ROOM

(GRANDPA, MOM, DAD, BILLY, and BETTY ENTER.)

MOM: See Grandpa, it's nice here and so peaceful.

DAD: Kids you stay here with Grandpa. Mom and I are going to find someone to talk to about registration.

MOM: *(pointing to CAPTIAN)* He looks important. *(MOM and DAD walk over to CAPTAIN.)*

GRANDPA: Kids don't look so sad. It looks nice here.

BILLY: Whatever! *(sulking)*

BETTY: Grandpa, why do you want to live here instead of with us? I can give you my room.

GRANDPA: *(coughs)* Darling, I don't think I can sleep with all your stuffed animals. I get a little claustrophobic. Besides, where would you sleep?

BILLY: This place is boring.

GRANDPA: Then I guess it's perfect! Sounds like they need me to liven' things up around here! *(starts to dance and loses balance)*

BILLY: *(helping him stand)* Grandpa!

GRANDPA: Kids I'm not as young as I used to be. My body is breaking down, and I don't want to be a burden on you youngins. Here, I can relax and not worry about things so much. They take care of you here.

(Just then a Lady SENIOR walks by and smiles at GRANDPA.)

GRANDPA: *(excitedly)* Oh, don't worry about your Grandpa! I'm going to make some nice friends here. *(winks at Lady Senior)* You just come and visit me often, and I'll be happy as a clam.

BETTY: *(giggling)* Grandpa! Let's go sit over there.

BILLY: Betty, you take Grandpa and find a seat, I'm going to go look around a bit.

EUGENE: *(shouting)* Pudding, when do we get our Pudding!

All SENIORS: Yeah! We want our pudding! Pudding!

STAFFER # 2: Calm dow. In a little while, Eugene.

GRANDPA: Wow, they must have really good pudding here. I hope it's chocolate.

SCENE 3

(ENTERS HONEY BEES.)
HONEY BEE LEADER: (*cheerleader like*) Ok girls make your rounds and then meet back here in 5 minutes. (*very serious*) Girls, remember one more week, and we get our Entertainment Service Badges. So let me see your smiles. That's it. Now go make someone happy!

(As the girls spread out and start to visit the SENIORS, STAFFERS begin to leave. MOM and DAD move over to where GRANDPA and BETTY are. HONEY BEE LEADER heads over to CAPTAIN.)

CAPTAIN: Now, remember to keep the volume of your singing low. We don't want to bother the other patients who are resting. Stay in this room. It's best to keep the doors closed at all times. You have 30 minutes, and that is all. Our seniors need their rest. We will be back in 30 minutes. Remember you have 30 minutes only.

GIRL SCOUT LEADER: (*talking fast*) Yes, sir. Thank you so much for letting us come. We are so excited to sing for our Seniors. Don't you think they love music? I think they love it. We really love singing for them. Do you think they have any special requests?

CAPTAIN: (*disgusted*) No! You have 30 minutes. (*He gestures to the Nursing staff and exists*)
   (*All the STAFFERS EXIT, except STAFFER #2 and an EXTRA STAFFER. The EXTRA STAFFER is finishing up with a Senior. The HONEYBEE GIRLS gather together. BILLY rushing back into the room, accidentally bumps into STAFFER #2, and falls down. He looks horrified.*)
STAFFER#2: Are you okay?
BILLY: (*stammering*) Uh, uh, uh (*cowers and blurts out*) Don't touch me!!
STAFFER#2: Ok, then. (*leaves*)
(*BILLY gets up and runs over to his MOM & DAD*)
BILLY: MOM, DAD!! (*out of breath*)
MOM: Billy, what's the matter?
DAD: Are you ok, son?
BILLY: Grandpa is in danger!
BETTY: What?
MOM: Billy, what are you talking about?
BILLY: I saw them. I saw it. They're putting something green in the Pudding; some kind of green ooze.
BETTY: Really?
MOM: Billy?
DAD: Billy, It's probably just medicine.
BILLY: No, I saw it. And I heard them talking. They said something

about the ship coming tomorrow at midnight with the full moon. They're aliens, Grandpa! They're aliens! We've got to get you out of here. They're going to take you.
MOM: Billy, this isn't funny. Stop it!
DAD: Now, Billy, we know you're not happy about Grandpa being here, but this is silly.
MOM: Honey, I think this might be too much for them.
BILLY: No, it's not!
MOM: Billy, keep your voice down! Grandpa?
GRANDPA: Billy, I'm going to be ok.
BILLY: Grandpa, you have to believe me!
BETTY: I believe you, Billy! Mom, I believe him.
BILLY: Grandpa?
GRANDPA: (*looking at MOM & DAD*) Billy, let's talk about this later. Okay?

(A HONEY BEE GIRL starts to play music for their camp song and the one STAFFER that didn't leave, suddenly horrified covers his/her ears and runs out screaming.)

BILLY: Did you see that? Betty, did you see that?
BETTY: Yeah! Weird, huh?

GRANDPA: Maybe their singing isn't very good? *(makes a face at BETTY who laughs)*
BETTY: Hey, I know that girl! She goes to my school.
(The HONEY BEE GIRLS sing a silly campy song. After the Song, the SENIORS applaud, and the girls go back to visiting the SENIORS. BETTY walks over to HONEY BEE LEADER.)
BETTY: Hey, that was really good. Aren't you in my science class?
HONEY BEE LEADER: Yeah! I know you, Betty, right?
BETTY: Yes.
HONEY BEE LEADER: We've been coming for a week now. We're getting our Entertainment Service Badge. Are you a Honey Bee?
BETTY: No
HONEY BEE LEADER: You should join! We have a lot of fun. Is that your grandfather?
BETTY: Yes, he's going to live here now. But my brother thinks aliens… um I mean something weird is going on here.
HONEY BEE LEADER: Did you say, aliens? Your brother is weird.
BETTY: Why did that guy freak out like that?
HONEY BEE LEADER: Yeah. Weird, huh? That happened the first day we came here and sang. It's like they don't

like our music or something? I don't know what their problem is. They're all kinds of weird here. None of the staff is allowed to stay and listen. Captain, the head guy, says they have things to do. Busy cleaning, I guess.

(The HONEY BEE GIRLS have all gathered at the door.)

BETTY: Oh, well, I better get back to my Grandpa. See you at school.

HONEY BEE LEADER: Okay. Here's my card, if you want to join. We're always looking for girls!

BETTY: Thanks!

(HONEY BEE LEADER joins the girls and they EXIT. After a minute, The STAFFERS ENTER with trays of pudding. The STAFFERS begin to pass them out to the SENIORS. CAPTAIN ENTERS and walks over to the family.)

CAPTIAN: I'm sorry visiting hours are over. It's time to say goodbye to Grandpa. We've got a room all ready for him. So you have no worries.

MOM: Thank you.

BILLY: No, Grandpa. You can't stay here. I'm telling the truth. *(glaring at Captain)* Something is going on here!

CAPTIAN: I can assure you, young man, there is nothing to worry about. Your Grandfather will be more than taken care of. It's time to leave.

STAFFER #3: (*handing Grandpa a cup of pudding*) Here's your pudding, Sir!

BILLY: No! Don't take that. *(knocks over the pudding)*

Everyone: (*chaotically everyone starts shouting*) NO! What! Pudding! Billy!

(The STAFFERS nearby quickly clean up the pudding mess. They act like he's just spilled toxic waste.)

DAD: (*pulls BILLY aside*) Billy! That's enough. What has come over you?

MOM: (*upset*) Grandpa, I think this is just too much for the kids. I think that this will be the last visit here for a while.

BETTY: No! Mom, what if he's right! What if aliens have taken over this place? The people here are very weird.

GRANDPA: Yeah, right! What if the kids are right? Aliens do come in all forms, you know.

MOM: Dad, don't be silly. Aliens have not taken over the nursing home.

BILLY: Grandpa, do you really believe me?

GRANDPA: I'm just saying it's possible.
BILLY: Grandpa, you've got to get evidence. You've got to get into the kitchen and get some of that ooze they're putting in the pudding. And don't eat any of it. Whatever you do, don't eat the pudding!
GRANDPA: I'll see what I can do, Billy. You be good, so you can come back and see me again, ok?
BILLY: Okay, Grandpa. Watch your back. Don't trust anyone.
GRANDPA: Promise me you'll be good! Promise?
BILLY: Promise!
BETTY: Grandpa, be careful. I'm starting to get a bad feeling.
(CAPTAIN begins to walk over with a look of resolution.)
DAD: We need to go, the Captain is coming, and he looks like he's going to lose his head if we don't leave now.
MOM: Wow, they're really strict here.
CAPTAIN: Excuse me, it's time for the Seniors to have some quiet time before they head to bed.
DAD: We're leaving right now, Sir. Sorry about the mess.
BILLY: (To CAPTAIN) We'll be back tomorrow!
BETTY: Yeah!
CAPTAIN: Can't wait.
(Waving Goodbye the FAMILY leaves GRANDPA for the night. CAPTAIN is standing there as they leave.)

SCENE 4

CAPTAIN: *(to STAFFER #3)* Keep an eye on him. I don't want that kid ruining our plans.
STAFFER #3: Yes, sir, very good Sir! *(he walks over to Grandpa with new pudding)* Here's your pudding, sir.
GRANDPA: I don't know if I'm very hungry now.
STAFFER #3: It's very important that you eat some, sir. It will relax you. All our Seniors love the pudding. Here! Have some sir.
EUGENE: I'll take his! Give it to me. *(starts to get up out of his seat to grab it)*
STAFFER #3: Sit down, Eugene! *(one of the Staffers comes over to handle Eugene)*
GRANDPA: Well, if it's that good. Hit me!
STAFFER #3: Very good sir! (gives the pudding to GRANDPA and walks away)

(GRANDPA, is beginning to wonder what is going on, pretends to eat the pudding to please the STAFFERS. When they're not looking, he gives his to EUGENE; who gulps it up. As the SENIORS finish their pudding, they begin to fall asleep. Some fall out of their seats, and the STAFFERS

drag them out. GRANDPA, having not eaten his doesn't fall asleep but pretends to sleep in his chair. After a pause, when GRANDPA thinks no one is looking, he gets up and walks off stage. After he EXITS, CAPTAIN, and STAFFER #3, and #2 come back in. CAPTAIN looks around the room to see how things are going. STAFFER #2 realizes GRANDPA is missing.)

STAFFER #2: Where's the new guy?

CAPTIAN: *(to his STAFFERS with urgency)* Find him. Now!

(As the STAFFERS begin to leave, they are met by STAFFER #4 and EXTRA STAFFERS who have GRANDFATHER by the arms. They present him to CAPTAIN.)

STAFFER #4: We found him in the kitchen, Sir. He had the Glook Sir.

(To GRANDPA'S amazement the STAFFERS (aliens) all begin to talk ALIEN Gibberish and gesture strangely frantically to one another.)

CAPTAIN: *(shouting)* Enough! I knew you, and that grandson of yours would be trouble.

GRANDPA: My grandson was right about you. You *are* aliens. When they come tomorrow, you and your friends will be discovered, and this charade of yours will be done for.

CAPTAIN: That's what you think, old man! *(laughs menacingly)* You humans, think you're alone in this universe. You're such small-minded creatures. After midnight tomorrow, you and your friends will be part of a New World Order, and you will see things with different eyes. You will become new recruits to our World Order. Your new purpose in life will be to serve us! Join us willingly or unwillingly, regardless you will serve. If you come without resistance and you will gain a position with The New Order. They will reward you in ways you could only imagine. Eat the pudding and join us! Be free from this feeble body and enjoy a new life as one of us! It is your choice. Either way, you are ours.

GRANDPA: Never! I may only be human, but I am loved here. My days may be numbered, but in the end, I will have lived a full life; a Human life. One of free will and love, not trapped in an alien form subject to your experiments and whatever your Order is.

CAPTAIN: Have it your way, old man. *(to the STAFFERS)* Take him to his room and lock him in there. Stand guard till the ship has arrived. One more dose of Glook and he will submit willingly.

(Staffers take Grandpa by the arms and EXIT.)

CAPTAIN: *(to the STAFFERS left behind)* Now for the grandson. *(He laughs menacingly)*

(DIM LIGHTS to represent the end of the day.)

SCENE 5
IT'S THE NEXT DAY.

(When the lights come on the nursing home is quiet. SENIORS and STAFFERS are sitting and walking around. GRANDPA is not there; his chair is empty. FAMILY ENTERS and look around for GRANDPA.)

BILLY: Where is Grandpa?
MOM: What room is he in?
DAD: I thought they told you.
MOM: *(looking in her purse)* They didn't tell me.
DAD: He told you! I know he told you.
MOM: Well, he didn't tell me, Dear!
DAD: Well, which room is he in?
MOM: I don't know that's why I asked you.
DAD: But I don't know, Dear!
BILLY: Mom, Dad, We've got to find him.
Betty: There's Eugene. Let's ask him. (points to EUGENE)
MOM: *(confused and looking around)* Where is that Captain fellow?
(BILLY & BETTY cross over to talk to EUGENE.)
BETTY: Mr. Eugene, have you seen my Grandfather? He was the new man that came yesterday?
BILLY: Do you know what room he's in?

EUGENE: Oh, yeah. The pudding guy! He gave me his pudding. I can't remember much after that. Pudding; Do you have some more pudding for me?

BILLY: He didn't eat the Pudding. (*pause*) They've taken him. Oh, no they've taken him.

    (CAPTAIN ENTERS with a few STAFFERS.)

BILLY: (*runs up to him*) Where's my Grandpa?

CAPTIAN: *(walks past BILLY to MOM & DAD)* I'm sorry. Grandpa has been very ill today. He came down with a bit of a bug late last night after you left. He won't be having visitors today. Come back tomorrow. I'm sure he'll be feeling better soon.

BETTY: What have you done with our Grandpa?

MOM: Betty, not you too! Billy, Betty, we'll come back tomorrow when Grandpa is feeling better. Come along, dear.

SCENE 6
HONEY BEES ENTER SINGING.

(STAFFERS covering and cowering they rush out of the room. CAPTAIN, covers his ears and shakes vigorously.)
CAPTAIN: *(speaks with great difficulty)* Excuse me. I've got to see to the…*(EXITS)*
BETTY: Why do they do that? That's so weird.
MOM: That was strange.
BILLY: I told you, mom. They're aliens. The singing! Their ears must be too sensitive to the singing. I've got an idea. Mom and Dad stay here and keep the girls singing.
BILLY: Betty and I will look for Grandpa.
(BILLY & BETTY EXIT in a rush off the stage.)
MOM: Dad, where did they go?
(When the girls finish their song, DAD approaches the girls to make the request. Before they can begin. CAPTIAN barges into the room with several STAFFERS who surround the HONEY BEE GIRLS.)
CAPTAIN: Girls! That's enough. Thank you. But it's time to leave.
HONEY BEE LEADER: But we haven't finished. We've had a request. We have to finish our service, or we

can't get our Entertainment Service Badges.
CAPTAIN: Enough, I said! Get them out of here.
   (The STAFFERS begin to round up the HONEY BEES.)
EUGENE: Where's my pudding!
STAFFER #3: Eugene, that's enough now.
ALL SENIORS: *(everyone all at once says something different)* What's going on here! Why did they stop singing? Let the girls sing! Where's the pudding? Nurse!
DAD: What's going on here?
MOM: Dad, go get Grandpa. This is no place for him.
   (BILLY, BETTY, and GRANDPA ENTER.)
BILLY: They had Grandpa, locked in his room.
DAD: How did you get by them?
BETTY: I sang a song!
MOM: Let's get out of here. These people are crazy!
BILLY: Mom, we can't just leave the others alone. They'll abduct them.
GRANDPA: It's true! The aliens are abducting them all, at midnight, tonight.
MOM: What can we do?
CAPTAIN: Now we'll have to take all of you! No one is allowed to leave. Round up the girls and the family!

(The STAFFERS gather up the HONEY BEE GIRLS and the FAMILY. STAFFERS line up on both sides of the stage to block everyone from leaving.)

BILLY: Quick, everyone, start singing! (BILLY grabs the music player and hits play)

(MUSIC cue)

(EVERYONE begins to sing a song. The STAFFERS all begin talking in alien gibberish and covering their ears. CAPTAIN shouts out a command in alien, and all the STAFFERS use their right hand and touch their ear. This seems to handle the singing. When EVERYONE realizes that the singing isn't working they all slowly stop singing.)

CAPTAIN: That won't work on us anymore. You stupid human! We're beginning to adapt to your sounds. We can resist you and your weak attempts to destroy our plans.

BILLY: Don't give up! Keep going. (He starts singing again)

(EVERYONE starts singing again this time with full force and dancing.)

BETTY: That's it! Louder! Louder everyone!

(To everyone's amazement EUGENE stands up and begins to sing in an Operatic voice! CAPTAIN and STAFFERS all collapse to the ground stunned from volume overload. At that, he

finishes his verse, and all the SENIORS applaud. The HONEY BEES cheer, and the FAMILY hugs.)

MOM: What just happened?
DAD: Are they dead?
BILLY: We should call the police.
GRANDPA: I think I'm going to like it here.
BETTY: Grandpa!

THE END

THE BANK JOB

Superheroes, with the help of a local news reporter, attempt to stop their archenemy from robbing the city bank.

CAST OF CHARACTERS:

SHELLY SNOOPER FROM INO NEWS – Has a cold

MAYOR SINGS-A-LOT – Breaks into song a lot

BRAIN GIRL – Superhero mind reader who can't read

CAPTAIN BUFF – Superhero strongman who is very sensitive

METAMORPHOSIS MAN – Superhero shapeshifter whose hard of hearing

DARK EVIL SHE-WHO-MUST-NOT-BE-NAMED VILLAIN –Who can walk through walls

*extras non-speaking town's people can be added.

SETTING:

This is a contemporary comedy that is set in a small town where superheroes exist.

LIST OF POSSIBLE PROPS:
- Signs that read: Bank Vault, Bank, Super Hero's Lair, Court House, Coffee Shop, and Wall
- Fake Money

- Notepad and paper
- Fake Laser
- Bag of Money
- Phone
- Super Hero Capes

NOTES:

This play is a comedy. I had a mix of students from 8-teen who really committed to their parts. The key to this play's success is a serious commitment to the characters. Get your kids to do that, and the audience will laugh wholeheartedly.

Metamorphosis Man –superpower is to Morph into things. He just rolls up into a ball or scrunches down into whatever he's trying to be. It adds to the humor of the scenes.

When Captain Buff has the others ride his back, we just had the kid lean and walk with him. It was really funny!

SCENE 1
TOWN HALL

(Scene begins with SHELLY SNOOPER interviewing the Town's mayor, MAYOR SINGS-A-LOT.)

SHELLY SNOOPER: *(sneezes)* Excuse me I have a really bad cold.

MAYOR SINGS-A-LOT: Here have a tissue *(sings)* "A person can develop a cold."

SHELLY SNOOPER: Thank you, *(sneezes)* Mayor Sings-A-Lot, can you tell us what the progress is with the city's budget?

MAYOR SINGS-A-LOT: *(sings)* "Money Money Money Ain't it funny! It's a rich man's world."

SHELLY SNOOPER: It's due tomorrow! Has the (sneezes) council reached a (sneezes) decision?

MAYOR SINGS-A-LOT: (sings) "Tomorrow. Tomorrow. I love ya, Tomorrow."

(ENTERS BRAIN GIRL.)

BRAIN GIRL: Mayor Sings-A-Lot! Mayor Sings-A-Lot! I'm sorry to interrupt you, but I must speak to you. It's an emergency!

MAYOR SINGS-A-LOT: Of course Brain Girl, *(sings)* "What's the buzz, tell me what's a-happenin'?"

SHELLY SNOOPER: Is it true, Brain Girl that you're a Super Hero with the power to read minds?
BRAIN GIRL: Yes, (*mind reads*) and Ah, no Shelly Snooper from INO News, I don't think you'd look better in my superhero outfit!
SHELLY SNOOPER: (*sneeze*) Wow, you really can read minds!
BRAIN GIRL: Mayor Sings-A-Lot, the Dark Evil She-who-must-not-be named Villain, is going to rob the City Bank and wipe out all the town's money.
SHELLY SNOOPER: The Dark Evil She-Who-Must-Not-Be-Named Villain is a notorious bank robber. (*sniff*) She has robbed banks all over the world, and now she is here? I hear she's notorious for her laugh. (*sniffs*) She can't stop laughing. (*sneeze*)
MAYOR SINGS-A-LOT: How does she do it? (sings) "Oh, this can't be happening." The budget is due tomorrow. We've got to stop her!
SHELLY SNOOPER: What's the plan?
BRAIN GIRL: I'll get my superhero friends, Captain Buff and Metamorphosis Man, and we'll come up with a plan to stop her!
MAYOR SINGS-A-LOT: (*sings*) "Heavy Heavy… this is so Heavy Baby" I'll go talk to the Chief of Police and

see what precautions we can get together.
BRAIN GIRL: (*receives mind read*) Oh, she's at the coffee shop.
SHELLY SNOOPER: Which coffee shop? (*sneezes*) The one on 6th, or Grand?
MAYOR SINGS-A-LOT: There's also the one on Main now, in the Corona Mall!
BRAIN GIRL: (*receives a mind read*) She's ordering a tall decaf Carmel Macchiato.
SHELLY SNOOPER: Yummy (*sneezes*)
MAYOR SINGS-A-LOT: (*frustrated*) Oh, never mind, I'll see to the Chief (*sings*) "Heavy Heavy, this is so Heavy Baby."

(MAYOR SINGS-A-LOT EXITS.)

BRAIN GIRL: To my friends! Up, out and away!

(BRAIN GIRL EXITS.)

SHELLY SNOOPER: I think I'll go get a cappuccino.

(BLACKOUT.)

SCENE 2
COFFEE SHOP

(SHELLY SNOOPER crosses to the coffee shop and waiting in line is DARK EVIL SHE-WHO-MUST-NOT-BE-NAMED VILLAIN.)

DARK EVIL SHE-WHO-MUST-NOT-BE-NAMED VILLAIN: Is this decaf? I asked for decaf, it better be decaf. I can't handle caffeine, and I have work to do! (*laughs*)

(SHELLY SNOOPER instantly knows it must be her from her laugh.)

SHELLY SNOOPER: Work? (*sneezes*) What work would that be? You wouldn't be the notorious Dark Evil She-Who-Must-Not-Be-Named Villain, would you?

DARK EVIL SHE-WHO-MUST-NOT-BE-NAMED VILLAIN: (*laughs*) Me (*laughs*) Now what makes you think that? Innocent me? (*laughs*) Do I look like a villain? (*laughs*) I've just come for a decaf Carmel Macchiato.

SHELLY SNOOPER: Yes, I see (*sniffs*) I must be mistaken. Then you wouldn't mind telling me your name now, would you? (*sneezes*)

DARK EVIL SHE-WHO-MUST-NOT-BE-NAMED VILLAIN: (*laughs*) I can't tell you that. (*laughs*)

SHELLY SNOOPER: Ah, ha! I knew it! I'm Shelly Snooper with INO news.

Would you mind answering a few questions?
DARK EVIL SHE-WHO-MUST-NOT-BE-NAMED VILLAIN: No, I'm sorry I must be going. I have to go to work. *(laughs)*
SHELLY SNOOPER: That wouldn't be robbing the city bank, would it?
DARK EVIL SHE-WHO-MUST-NOT-BE-NAMED VILLAIN: *(laughs)* Sorry I don't know what you're talking about. *(quickly gathers her things)* Besides if I was the Dark Evil She-Who-Must-Not-Be-Named Villain, how could I do such a thing? Rob the city bank, really! *(laughs)*
SHELLY SNOOPER: Are you aware that the city budget is due to be voted on tomorrow? If all the money in the city bank is stolen, the city will go bankrupt.
DARK EVIL SHE-WHO-MUST-NOT-BE-NAMED VILLAIN: *(laughs)* Pity really! I think the only way someone would be able to get away with robbing the city bank is if they could walk through walls. *(laughs)*
  (DARK EVIL SHE-WHO-MUST-NOT-BE-NAMED VILLAIN EXITS by walking through the wall of the coffee shop.)
SHELLY SNOOPER: *(frantically looking around)* Did anyone see that? She just walked through the wall. I've got to tell Major Sings-A-Lot.
        (SHELLY SNOOPER EXITS.)

SCENE 3
SUPERHERO HIDEOUT

(Meanwhile, back in the Superhero hideout BRAIN GIRL, CAPTAIN BUFF, and METAMORPHOSIS MAN are discussing options on how to stop DARK EVIL SHE-WHO-MUST-NOT-BE-NAMED VILLAIN.)

BRAIN GIRL: So you see we've got to come up with a plan to stop The Dark Evil She-Who-Must-Be-Named Villain, or the City Bank will be robbed, and the city will go bankrupt.

CAPTAIN BUFF: Bankrupt? Oh, no. *(cries)*

METAMORPHOSIS MAN: Heads up? *(trying to hear)* What did you say?

BRAIN GIRL: I said, *(holding his head between her hands so he can read her lips)* The Dark Evil She-Who-Must-Not-Be-Named Villain is going to rob the City Bank unless we do something about it.

CAPTAIN BUFF: *(big sob)*

BRAIN GIRL: *(getting mad)* Where are your hearing aids?

METAMORPHOSIS MAN: *(pointing to CAPTAIN BUFF)* He crushed them. I had him hold them while I morphed into a stop sign this morning to avoid a car accident.

CAPTAIN BUFF: (*starts to cry again*) Oh okay! Bring that up now, at a time like this.
BRAIN GIRL: Can we focus on the plan?
METAMORPHOSIS MAN: Oh, I know I'll morph into a bag of money and wait out in the bank vault. When she tries to take me, I'll morph back into me and surprise her!
CAPTAIN BUFF: That's such a good idea! (*sniffs, starting to feel better*) I know! When you surprise her, I'll rip the vault door open, jump out and grab her so she can't get away.
BRAIN GIRL: That's good. Then I'll "Ah-ha her"! (wink wink)
    (*BRAIN GIRL and CAPTAIN BUFF both giggle.*)
METAMORPHOSIS MAN: What'd he say? (*to BRAIN GIRL*)
BRAIN GIRL: (*loudly in his face*) He likes your idea!
METAMORPHOSIS MAN: Ok, so after I surprise her, Captain Buff, you can grab her.
CAPTAIN BUFF: That's what I said!
METAMORPHOSIS MAN: What'd you say? (*to CAPTAIN BUFF*)
CAPTAIN BUFF: I said that I'd grab her after you surprised her and Brain Girl will "Ah-ha" her.

METAMORPHOSIS MAN: Well it doesn't make sense for you to grab her until *after* I surprise her.
CAPTAIN BUFF: That's what I said. *(starting to get upset)*
METAMORPHOSIS MAN: *(getting mad)* Fine, have it your way! If you think you can morph into money to lure her, go ahead. I'd like to see you try!
CAPTAIN BUFF: Why are you getting so upset? This is very upsetting. *(cries)*
BRAIN GIRL: Don't worry, Captain Buff it'll be ok. *(to METAMORPHOSIS MAN)* Well, go with the original plan.
METAMORPHOSIS MAN: Which plan is that?
(ENTERS MAYOR SINGS-A-LOT and SHELLY SNOOPER.)
MAYOR SINGS-A-LOT: *(sings)* "We have some news" on the Dark Evil She-Who-Must-Not-Be-Named Villain.
SHELLY SNOOPER: *(excitedly)* I've discovered that she can walk through walls. *(Sneeze)* That's how she gets into the banks.
CAPTAIN BUFF: Oh yeah, we knew that.
SHELLY SNOOPER: Oh! *(deflated)* How?
BRAIN GIRL: The Dark Evil She-Who-Must-Not-Be-Named Villain used to be one of us until we discovered her

weakness, and she got angry and left.
SHELLY SNOOPER: What's her weakness?
METAMORPHOSIS MAN: What's going on?
BRAIN GIRL: *(to METAMORPHOSIS MAN)* Why don't you practice your morphing?
(METAMORPHOSIS MAN begins practicing morphing into different shapes.)
CAPTAIN BUFF: Her name is her weakness.
SHELLY SNOOPER: You know her true name?
BRAIN GIRL: Yes, but I'm sorry that's classified information.
MAYOR SINGS-A-LOT: *(frantic)* "What's the buzz tell me what's a-happenin'? What's the buzz?"
SHELLY SNOOPER: So then what's the plan, mighty Superhero friends?
BRAIN GIRL: Metamorphosis Man is going to morph into a bag of money and wait out in the vault for the Dark Evil She-Who-Must-Not-Be-Named Villain to try and take him. Then he'll surprise her and Captain Buff will then rip open the vault door and grab her while I "Ah-ha" her into giving up. Then we'll turn her over to the police.
SHELLY SNOOPER: "Ah-ha" her?
BRAIN GIRL: Sorry that's highly classified too!
SHELLY SNOOPER: Okay?

BRAIN GIRL: Wait, incoming! *(receives a mind read)* She is on her way to the bank now. We've got to get going.

MAYOR SINGS-A-LOT: *(freaking out)* What are we all doing here? Let's "Move on down, move on down the road."

CAPTAIN BUFF: Everyone on my back, I can run us all over! *(to METAMORPHOSIS MAN's face)* Metamorphosis Man seat belt! (METAMORPHOSIS MAN morphs into a seat belt) Brain Girl lead the way!

BRAIN GIRL: Ah, ah *(stammers)* Which direction is it in?

SHELLY SNOOPER: You don't know where the bank is?

BRAIN GIRL: I do, but I seem to always get myself lost somehow.

MAYOR SINGS-A-LOT: I'll lead the way. *(sings)* "Ease on down, ease on down the road!"

(They all EXIT the stage.)

SCENE 4
BANK VAULT

(DARK EVIL SHE-WHO-MUST-NOT-BE-NAMED VILLAIN is in the bank vault. She rummages around the vault looking at all the money sitting around like it's candy in a candy store laughing to herself. She then pulls out a key in her pocket and opens up a safety deposit box. She rummages around the box only to find she has forgotten to include her laser to break out of the Vault with the money.)

DARK EVIL SHE-WHO-MUST-NOT-BE-NAMED VILLAIN: Where is my laser? *(jumping up and down like a child)* Stupid! Stupid! Stupid! *(throws up her arms)* Of all the things to forget. (has a second thought) Maybe? *(desperate she makes several unsuccessful attempts to take a bag of money through the wall with her, but the money won't go through the other side)* Augh! Fine. *(laughs)* I'll just have to go back to the lab and get the laser and come back again. (defeated *she puts back the box and places the bag of money back in place and walks through the wall of the vault)*

(DARK EVIL SHE-WHO-MUST-NOT-BE-NAMED VILLAIN EXITS the stage.)

SCENE 5
OUTSIDE THE BANK

(The group arrived at the bank METAMORPHOSIS MAN release them from his seat belt frame, and un-morphs, and then CAPTAIN BUFF lets them down).

SHELLY SNOOPER: This is the luckiest day of my career (*sneezes*) and to think that I almost called in sick.

BRAIN GIRL: (*mind read*) the Dark Evil She-Who-Must-Not-Be-Named Villain was here, but now she's gone. She'll be back again. We should hurry and get into place before we miss our opportunity.

MAYOR SINGS-A-LOT: The Bank Manager texted me the instructions for getting into the vault. He'd do it for you, but he doesn't want to upset the customers into thinking there's a problem; here Brain Girl take this with you.

METAMORPHOSIS MAN: What's that?

BRAIN GIRL: It's the directions on getting into the vault.

METAMORPHOSIS MAN: Directions on making a malt?

BRAIN GIRL: No, the vault!

METAMORPHOSIS MAN: Oh, let's go to the vault and get this over with. She should be on her way by now.

CAPTAIN BUFF: Mayor Sings-A-Lot and Shelly Snooper, you both, should stay here; it might get… dangerous
MAYOR SINGS-A-LOT: "Highway to the Danger Zone."
(MAYOR SINGS-A-LOT and SHELLY SNOOPER EXIT.)

SCENE 6
INSIDE THE VAULT

BRAIN GIRL: *(mind read)* Quickly she's on her way back, oh no, she dropped something, no she picks it up, no she forgot something else. Oh, no she's on the way. Yes, she's on the way.
CAPTAIN BUFF: This is nerve-racking.
METAMORPHOSIS MAN: Open the vault.
CAPTAIN BUFF: (begins to take the door off.)
BRAIN GIRL: No, we have to do it the right way. You know with the directions.
(BRAIN GIRL stands in front of the vault keypad. Looking at the directions and the pad and back at the directions and at the pad again.)
METAMORPHOSIS MAN: What's the problem?
BRAIN GIRL: I can't do it.
CAPTAIN BUFF: What's the matter?
BRAIN GIRL: I can't read it.
CAPTAIN BUFF: Is the writing too small? Oh, I always have problems with texts when the font is small.
METAMORPHOSIS MAN: We don't have time for this. What's the matter?
BRAIN GIRL: *(bursts out crying)* I CAN'T READ. I CAN'T READ AT ALL. I CAN'T READ THE INSTRUCTIONS.

CAPTAIN BUFF: *(comforts BRAIN GIRL)* Oh, it'll be all right. There, there now.
(SHELLY SNOOPER ENTERS.)
SHELLY SNOOPER: You can read minds, but you can't read words? *(writes it down)* Wow!
BRAIN GIRL: I thought we told you to stay out of there?
CAPTAIN BUFF: It can get dangerous.
SHELLY SNOOPER: Yeah, but this is where the story is.
METAMORPHOSIS MAN: We don't have time for this. Give that to me already. *(Takes the cell phone from BRAIN GIRL and uses it to open the Vault door)*
CAPTAIN BUFF: *(to SHELLY SNOOPER)* Get back and stay out of the way.
(They ENTER the vault.)
BRAIN GIRL: *(mind reads)* She's outside the bank. Hurry!
(METAMORPHOSIS MAN morphs into a bag of money, and CAPTAIN BUFF, BRAIN GIRL, and SHELLY SNOOPER leave the vault and shut the door behind them, and wait outside the door. The DARK EVIL SHE-WHO-MUST-NOT-BE-NAMED VILLAIN walks through the bank wall into the vault. Looks around the vault. She grabs some jewels and money she finds, laying around, and stuffs them in her pockets. Then she grabs METAMORPHOSIS MAN thinking

he's a bag of money and drags him to the wall. She then points a laser at the wall and METAMORPHOSIS MAN jumps up in his human form.)
METAMORPHOSIS MAN: Surprise. You won't get away this time.
DARK EVIL SHE-WHO-MUST-NOT-BE-NAMED VILLAIN: *(laughs)*
(BRAIN GIRL signals CAPTAIN BUFF, and he rips the vault door off, and BRAIN GIRL rushes in.)
BRAIN GIRL: "Ah-ha" Petunia Plum! You're not going to get away this time.
DARK EVIL SHE-WHO-MUST-NOT-BE-NAMED VILLAIN: No, not my real name!!! How could you?
(CAPTAIN BUFF grabs DARK EVIL SHE-WHO-MUST-NOT-BE-NAMED VILLAIN from behind.)
CAPTAIN BUFF: You're not getting away this time.
(MAYOR SINGS-A-LOT rushes in)
MAYOR SINGS-A-LOT: You did it. You're not "Getting away, getting away, getting away, now."
SHELLY SNOOPER: The DARK EVIL SHE-WHO-MUST-NOT-BE-NAMED VILLAIN real name is Petunia Plum? No wonder you don't want people to know that. How embarrassing. (writes it down)
DARK EVIL SHE-WHO-MUST-NOT-BE-NAMED VILLAIN: No no no, you can't publish that. *(laughs)* I'll get you for

this. I'll get you all for this.
(laugh)
(DARK EVIL SHE-WHO-MUST-BE-NAMED VILLAIN throws up the money and jewels she had stashed in her clothes. MAYOR SINGS-A-LOT drops to her knees and gathering the spilled money up in his arms. Knocking over BRAIN GIRL who bumps into SHELLY SNOOPER. Everyone begins to speak all at once.)

BRAIN GIRL: Everybody, calm down! Mayor Sings-A-Lot don't panic!

MAYOR SINGS-A-LOT: The money! The city's money! The budget. The money.

SHELLY SNOOPER: Petunia Plum, how do you spell that?

METAMORPHOSIS MAN: What about Plums? Did someone say we're having plums?

CAPTAIN BUFF: *(Releasing his grip)* This is so out of control. *(starts crying)* I just can't take it anymore. *(While everyone is scrambling around on the floor either trying to pick up the money or trying to get up from getting pushed over. DARK EVIL SHE-WHO-MUST-NOT-BE-NAMED VILLAIN quietly slips out from the commotion and quickly escapes through the wall.)*

DARK EVIL SHE-WHO-MUST-NOT-BE-NAMED VILLAIN: *(laughs)* Looks like I got away this time.

THE END

CINDERELLA...REVISITED!

Cinderella's enchanted shoe not only turns the Kingdom upside down looking for its owner, but is also responsible for a missing prince and a curious-looking mouse.

CAST OF CHARACTERS:
CINDERELLA
MOUSE/PRINCE CHARMING
STEPMOTHER
ANASTASIA (step-sister)
DRUSILLA (step-sister)
ROYAL STEWARD

SETTING:
 This fairy tale takes place in the home of Cinderella's stepmother. There are three rooms; Cinderella's bedroom basement, Anastasia & Drusilla's room, and the main hall.

LIST OF POSSIBLE PROPS:
- Shoe
- Chair
- brush

NOTES:
 This is a very silly play when done well. It can be very entertaining. Especially if the kids really commit to the characters.

SCENE 1
CINDERELLA'S BASEMENT ROOM

(Scene opens with CINDERELLA and MOUSE (PRINCE CHARMING) sitting near the fireplace.)

CINDERELLA: For heaven's sake, why did you follow me, your Highness?

PRINCE CHARMING: You left so suddenly, you forgot to tell me your name.

CINDERELLA: Then you grabbed my shoe! I should have told you it was enchanted. I had no idea that you would be turned into a mouse.

PRINCE CHARMING: I don't think it would've made a difference. Really, I can be very determined when I want something.

CINDERELLA: I've been trying to get a hold of my Fairy God Mother, but I think she's on vacation or something. She's just unreachable. But don't worry; I have every woodland creature on the lookout. I do hope you don't mind staying here with me. I couldn't just leave you there. I wouldn't want anything to happen to you.

PRINCE CHARMING: Well, at least I learned your name.

CINDERELLA: Funny, you'd think that you'd be smaller as a mouse!

PRINCE CHARMING: Don't remind me. What am I, 2 feet tall! I don't look like a mouse at all. I look more like an overgrown swamp rat.
CINDERELLA: Yes, it does make it difficult for me to hide you.
STEPMOTHER: Cinderella!
CINDERELLA: Oh, no, it's my Stepmother. Oh, how she hates mice.
PRINCE CHARMING: Where should I go?
   (Just then the door opens.)
CINDERELLA: (she *grabs the PRINCE/MOUSE and whispers*) hold still, don't move.
   (STEPMOTHER ENTERS.)
STEPMOTHER: (*sees the MOUSE*) Augh! What's that?
CINDERELLA: Oh, it's my new stuffed animal. Do you like it? I call it my Prince Charming.
STEPMOTHER: (*repulsed*) My child, maybe you've been down here a little too long for your own good. (*stern*) Come upstairs. We need you to help us get ready. The Royal Steward is on his way here.
PRINCE CHARMING: (*blurts out*) For me?
STEPMOTHER: (*mistaking him for CINDERELLA*) Don't be ridiculous my dear! I think the Prince has enough servants of his own, why would he want you too?
CINDERELLA: Yes, Stepmother.

STEPMOTHER: Get upstairs now! And hurry, we have no time to waste. He'll arrive at any moment.
CINDERELLA: (*starts to pick up the MOUSE*) This is our chance.
STEPMOTHER: What are you doing?
CINDERELLA: Oh, um
STEPMOTHER: Leave that thing here!
CINDERELLA: Yes, Step-Mother. (*turns to whisper*) I'll come back to you when I can. Be on the lookout for Fairy Godmother.
 (*They EXIT leaving PRINCE CHARMING behind.*)

(*BLACKOUT*)

SCENE 2
ANASTASIA & DRUSILLA'S BEDROOM

(Scene begins with CINDERELLA working on DRUSILLA's hair.)

ANASTASIA: Mother, hasn't she helped Drusilla enough! I need help with my dress. Just look at this ruffle?

STEPMOTHER: Cinderella! Help Anastasia.

DRUSILLA: But mother, my hair isn't perfect.

STEPMOTHER: It'll have to do; he'll be here at any moment.

(The DOORBELL rings)

ANASTASIA & DRUSILLA: Cinderella! Hurry, get this! Don't touch that. Stop that!

STEPMOTHER: Girls, that's enough! Come with me and put on your best smiles. He's here.

CINDERELLA: May I go now, Step-Mother?

STEPMOTHER: Oh, yes, stay out of the main hall unless I call you. Do you understand me, Cinderella? I don't want to hear a peep from you unless I call.

CINDERELLA: Yes, Stepmother.

(CINDERELLA EXITS then the STEPMOTHER & SISTERS EXIT.)

SCENE 3
MAIN HALL

(STEPMOTHER gracefully welcomes the ROYAL STEWARD into the room.)

STEPMOTHER: Your Grace.

ROYAL STEWARD: Madam, I'm here on a very official matter. The Prince has been missing since the ball. We must find him.

ANASTASIA & DRUSILLA: Oh no, the prince!!!

STEPMOTHER: What can we do to help your Grace?

ROYAL STEWARD: As you and your daughters attended the ball, you may have noticed that the prince spent most of the night with one young lady in particular. Unfortunately, no one knows who she is. This glass shoe is all we have to go by. It is my duty, to have every maiden in the kingdom try on this shoe so that we may attempt to find out who she is. The Prince may be out looking for her.

STEPMOTHER: What a burden has been put upon you sir. Please sit, relax, let us make you more comfortable.

(The GIRLS direct him to a chair, he sits, and STEPMOTHER begins to massage his shoulders.)

ROYAL STEWARD: *(relaxes)* Awe that's so nice! *(suddenly realizes how*

inappropriate it is) Oh, well, excuse me. *(stands up quickly)* I must get down to business. If this girl is the Prince's true love, they must be married at once.
ANASTASIA & DRUSILLA: *(excited)* Oh!!!
STEPMOTHER: Yes, of course, Your Grace. Anastasia, come here and try on this shoe.
ANASTASIA: *(taking the shoe to look at)* Oh, this looks just like my shoe.
DRUSILLA: *(grabbing at the shoe)* No, it's my shoe!
ANATASIA: Mother!!!! It's my shoe, you little twit!
DRUSILLA: *(they begin to fight)* We'll see about that!
ROYAL STEWARD: *(terrified the shoe will break, he takes the shoe back.)* No ladies, one at a time.
STEPMOTHER: Anastasia. *(sticks her tongue out at Drusilla)*
ANASTASIA: Yes, mother. *(sits to let the ROYAL STEWART attempt to try on her shoe. It is quite the commotion. The shoe doesn't fit at all.)* Oh no, my feet must be swollen from dancing all night at the ball.
DRUSILLA: It's my turn, bigfoot! I told you it was mine.
(Disappointed ANASTASIA gets up to let DRUSILLA sit down to try on the shoe.)

DRUSILLA: See I told you it was my shoe. Oh, wait, don't push so hard! Stop that. Let me do it!
ROYAL STEWARD: That is enough. It does not fit. Are there any other young ladies in the house?
STEPMOTHER: Only myself Your Grace. Maybe I could have a try.
ANASTASIA & **DRUSILLA:** Mother?
ROYAL STEWARD: (*Too tired to protest agrees*) Fine, but might I have a cup of tea?
STEPMOTHER: But of course. CINDERELLA!!!

          (BLACKOUT)

SCENE 4
MAIN HALL

(CINDERELLA ENTERS.)
CINDERELLA: *(timidly)* Yes, Step-Mother?
STEPMOTHER: Get his grace a cup of tea. Please rest Your Grace.
ROYAL STEWARD: *(suddenly realizes CINDERELLA is a beautiful young maiden)* Wait. Come try on this shoe, my lady.
ANASTASIA & DRUSILLA & STEPMOTHER: (shocked) Cinderella?
ANASTASIA: She is our servant.
DRUSILLA: Scullery maid.
STEPMOTHER: She is but a commoner Your Grace. Away Cinderella!
CINDERELLA: Yes, Step-Mother.
ROYAL STEWARD: My orders are that *every* young maiden in the kingdom. *(takes her by the hand)* Come sit down.
(With everyone waiting breathlessly, the ROYAL STEWARD leans down to have CINDERELLA try on the glass slipper when suddenly the PRINCE CHARMING enters in his mouse form, terrifying the ROYAL STEWARD, who falls over breaking the glass slipper.)
EVERYONE: *(screams)* Augh! What's that? Get it! Help!
ROYAL STEWARD: The slipper! *(bends over crying)*

CINDERELLA: (*turns to see the ROYAL PRINCE in Mouse form*) Your Highness.
STEPMOTHER: She's lost her mind.
ROYAL STEWARD: Did she just call him "Your highness?"
STEPMOTHER: (*to the steward*) Your grace, she is unwell.
PRINCE CHARMING: Steward!
DRUSILLA & ANASTASIA: (*look at each other and both faint, falling over each other.*)
ROYAL STEWARD: (*recognizing his voice*) It can't be! Your Highness?
PRINCE CHARMING: (*carrying the other slipper skips over and places the other shoe on CINDERELLA's foot, it fits and he magically transformed into himself again.*)
ROYAL STEWARD: (*amazed*) Your Highness!
STEPMOTHER: It can't be?
CINDERELLA: (*to the prince*) How did you know?
PRINCE CHARMING: Your little mouse friends suggested that if I was turned into a mouse because I took off your shoe, I might try putting it back on to change back. I thought it couldn't hurt to try.
ROYAL STEWARD: Your Highness, the King, is very worried we should return to him at once and explain what happened.

PRINCE CHARMING: First there is a matter of announcing that this fair maiden, my Cinderella, is my true love and we will be joined in marriage at once. That is if she'll have me.
STEPMOTHER: (*gasps*)
DRUSILLA & ANASTASIA: (*having regained consciousness upon hearing this faint again*)
CINDERELLA: Your Highness, my love, of course, I will be yours!
   (*They embrace, and then they turn around to EXIT when we notice that the PRINCE still has a tail!*)
ROYAL STEWARD: (*announces*) And they live Happily Ever After…

THE END

ALIEN HALLOWEEN

Jennifer isn't about to let two uninvited alien visitors from another planet stop her from having the party of the year!

CAST OF CHARACTERS

NARRATOR* (could be a possible voice-over)
TONK – alien 1
TOOKIE – alien 2
JENNIFER WHITE– party hostess
ELLEN FRANK– Jennifer's best friend
BEN WHITE– Jennifer's little brother
STACEY – popular cheerleader
TRICIA SPENSER - popular cheerleader
PRINCESS TOLSKA – alien princess
*party attendees could be added as extras

SETTING

This is a contemporary play that takes place today. There are two locations: planet Marsha and the earthly home of Jennifer White on Halloween night.

POSSIBLE LIST OF PROPS
- breakable telephone
- tray of food
- punch bowl or pitcher

- Alien device

NOTES

    It is possible to add extras party attendees if there is a need for more players.

    Left stage entrance/exit is to the living room. Right stage entrance/exit is to the kitchen door. Everything in the White's House takes place in the kitchen.

SCENE 1
PLANET MARSHA

NARRATOR: (*In a twilight zone voice*) In a universe as wide as eternity we assume we are alone. Welcome to the planet Marsha, only a few light-years from earth, home of Tonk and Tookie. Tonk has just received the call to Rama, the Marshian coming of age journey. When a Marshian reaches the age of maturity, they are sent on a mission to explore another world, where they learn by their own experience, to appreciate what Marshian life has to offer.
TONK: (*hunched over some kind of device*)
TOOKIE: (*excitedly*) Tonk, Tonk, Tonk we have received orders.
TONK: Tookie I am in the middle of interlocking the biometric ray to the ….
TOOKIE: (*interrupting*) Tonk, we have received orders for Rama.
TONK: (*stands up*) Rama!
TOOKIE: We are going to Earth.
TONK & TOOKIE: Earth! Earth! Earth!
  (*TONK and TOOKIE jump up and down excitedly. TONK then Pauses while TOOKIE continues to jump up and down then sits down disappointed.*)
TONK: I don't want to go to Earth.

TOOKIE: Earth has a lot of technology you could explore. I would think that you could not wait to go and see for yourself.

TONK: (*anxious*) Earth is covered with water. The planet is made up of nearly 70% water. We evaporate in the water! They have water everywhere. It falls from the sky. They use it to eat with, to clean with, and they purposely go into it and cover their bodies with it. (*freaking out*) We will evaporate and die.

TOOKIE: Tonk Tonk Tonk. Many others have traveled to earth before us and returned. We will wear protective suits that will keep us dry, and if we come into contact with water, we will not evaporate. I want to go. I want to explore earthly sound waves. They call it mus--ac. They have a custom called dancing. I will learn how to dance on Earth and get "jiggy with it." (*tries to dance*)

TONK: I suppose I would like to learn more about what they call TV. I have seen a few of the broadcasts on the erector scene. They have a human named (*swoons*) Brad Pitt that I would like to meet. He is a very pretty human.

TOOKIE: Then we accept the call to Rama and go to Earth? (sticks out a hand to shake)
TONK: (shakes hand back) Agreed. We go to Earth.

(BLACKOUT)

SCENE 2
ON EARTH AT JENNIFER WHITE'S HOUSE

NARRATOR: Back on Earth, Jennifer White and her best friend Ellen Frank, innocently discuss tonight's Halloween party. They have no idea that their lives are about to change forever. For what it means to be human will never be the same after tonight's encounter with another world.
JENNIFER: Do you think I've got enough food?
ELLEN: Only if your planning on feeding the entire school.
JENNIFER: Do you think I should make more punch?
ELLEN: Jennifer, calm down it's fine. Besides, haven't you already exceeded your budget?
JENNIFER: That was before I knew that the most popular girls in school were coming. What are they going to think of me if I don't have enough dip?
ELLEN: Does it really matter what they think?
JENNIFER: Yes! Ellen, we're only sophomores, and it's a huge compliment for seniors to even consider coming to an underclassman's party. Especially since cheer tryouts are coming up

next month. I asked Trisha Spenser, the captain of the cheerleading squad to come, and she said, "yes." If I can get on her good side, then maybe I can make the squad.

ELLEN: If you think that will make a difference. Shouldn't your talent be enough to qualify you for the squad? (Looking out the kitchen window) Hey, what's that light?

JENNIFER: What? (*too busy to look*)

ELLEN: (*frightened*) Jennifer is that what I think it is?

JENNIFER: (*finally looks up to see and can't believe what she's seeing*) It's probably just my little brother playing a practical joke.

ELLEN: Jennifer, that's some joke. It looks like a UFO just landed in your backyard. The door is opening. Jennifer, look at that!

JENNIFER: (*speechless*) What? (There's a knock at her kitchen door. Starts freaking out.) This can't be happening! (There's another knock at the kitchen door.)

ELLEN: Are you going to answer that?

JENNIFER: No! No way! I can't deal with this right now. I've got a party to attend too. (There's another knock at the door.)

JENNIFER: (*yells*) Sorry, no one is home. Go away. Come back tomorrow.

ELLEN: This is too good to be true.(let themselves in.)
TONK: Hello, I am Tonk. We are from the planet, Marsha.
ELLEN: This is the coolest thing that's ever happened to me. We should go tell your parents.
JENNIFER: No, don't you dare.
TOOKIE: I am Tookie. Do you have music?
TONK: Or Brad Pit?
ELLEN: Brad Pit?
JENNIFER: I'm sorry you're going to have to leave. I'm having a party, and my guests are about to arrive.
    (Front Door Bell rings.)
ELLEN: Too late!
JENNIFER: Argh, they're here, what am I going to do?
TONK: Water! Tookie I detect water in proximity. Water! Water! Water!
ELLEN: Do you want something to drink? (*Crosses to kitchen sink to pour a glass of water.*)
TOOKIE: No, No, No, we do not drink water. Water makes us evaporate.
  (*Front doorbell rings again.*)
JENNIFER: (*freaking out*) Stay here, I'll go answer the door. (*to ELLEN*) Hide them.
  (*JENNIFER EXIT and BEN ENTERS from another way.*)
BEN: Hey, Ellen! Is anyone going to answer the door?

ELLEN: Jennifer just went to get it. (*TONK and TOOKIE can't help but explore everything. Opening and closing things, taking apart the telephone, and even examining ELLEN's hair and clothes.*)
ELLEN: Stop that.
BEN: (*observing the aliens*) Wow, cool costumes.
TONK: Costume? What is a costume?
ELLEN: Ben this is Tonk and Tookie from the planet Marsha. Tonk put the phone back together.
BEN: Cool!
ELLEN: Have some finger food. Some real brain food!
TONK: (*to TOOKIE*) They eat fingers for food?
TOOKIE: Brain Food? I did not know that humans were cannibals?
BEN: (*laughs, thinking it's a joke*) Good one!
(*JENNIFER ENTERS.*)
JENNIFER: Ben, what are you doing down here?
BEN: What? Can't I have something to eat?
(*TONK and TOOKIE are picking up and smelling all the food.*)
JENNIFER: What are they still doing here?
BEN: Wow, maybe I don't want to come to your party.

JENNIFER: They're aliens Ben! Aliens landed in the backyard, and they're here inside our house on the most important night of my life.
BEN: Jennifer, are you sure you're not taking this party thing a little too seriously?
(ELLEN grabs BEN by the arm and shows him the spaceship out the window.)
ELLEN: They're real!
BEN: No way! I'm going to get Mom and Dad!
(Starts to take off when JENNIFER grabs him by the collar.)
JENNIFER: Don't you dare! I'll kill you if you tell them. We're going to have the best party of the year, and nothing is going to stop us. After the party is over, if they're still here, then you can go tell them. Until then… (*thinks about it for a moment*) They're just guests, dressed up as aliens. Yeah! Ellen, you and Ben are the only ones who know. Don't tell anyone. Ellen, you stay by Tonk and Ben you stay with the other one.
ELLEN: Tookie.
JENNIFER: Whatever. Just don't let them out of your sight. I'll keep the cheerleaders away from them.

ELLEN: Tonk. Tookie. Come with us, and we'll show you the rest of the house.
TONK: (*excited*) Tonk see Brad Pit?
TOOKIE: (*jumping up and down*) Tookie want to Dance.
BEN: Good thing, we got a DJ!
(They all EXIT.)

SCENE 3
JENNIFER WHITE'S KITCHEN

(Sometime later JENNIFER, TRICIA, and STACEY ENTER the kitchen to look for some food.)

JENNIFER: And here we have some food. Help yourselves! Let me know if there's anything else I can get you.

(A crash sound from the other room grabs her attention)

JENNIFER: I better see what that was. I'll be right back.
TRICIA: Thanks. (*unimpressed*)
(JENNIFER EXITS.)
STACEY: How long do we have to stay here? I'm so bored. Tell me why we agreed to come?
TRICIA: I don't know. You have to admit she certainly went all out. Look outside. Is that a spaceship? This family really loves Halloween.
STACEY: How many calories are in a popcorn ball?
TRICIA: Too many!
(BEN and TOOKIE ENTER.)
BEN: Hello, ladies! Can I help you with something?
TACEY: Aren't you a little young to be here?
BEN: Looks can be deceiving.
TOOKIE: (*walks up to TRICIA, she's dressed like a vampire*) *and pulls*

her lip up) Do you wear fangs for drinking blood also?
TRICIA: What are you doing?
BEN: Tookie, come with me.
(BEN grabs TOOKIE and begins to take her into the other room away from the girls.)
TOOKIE: Earth is very strange. Do many humans have superhero powers? What are wings for, if you don't fly?
BEN: Tookie! It's Halloween. They're just dressed up in costumes for fun. Let's try dancing again.
(TOOKIE begins to dance all crazy as BEN leads her out JENNIFER ENTERS.)
JENNIFER: Sorry about that.
(ELLEN ENTERS with TONK.)
ELLEN: Jennifer, you might want to help out here.
JENNIFER: (*to the cheerleaders*) Excuse me. (t*o ELLEN*) What now?
ELLEN: Tonk just eat some candy, and we'll look…
(TONK is talking nonsense and running around like mad freaking out the Cheerleaders.)
STACEY: What is wrong with you.
TONK: Tonk like candy. More candy.
JENNIFER: (*grabbing TONK by the arm*) No more candy. Please, Ellen, take it out of here.
(TONK and ELLEN EXIT.)

TRICIA: Wow, you got some kind of wild UFO theme going on here. (*looking out the window*) Do you guys do that every Halloween?

JENNIFER: (*nervous*) Um, well, this year is special, I guess.

TRICIA: (*impressed*) Well it is kind of cool. I wish my family went all out like this on Halloween.

JENNIFER: Thanks. What kind of music do you like? You can ask the DJ to put on anything you like. Here, let me introduce you to him.

STACEY: He was kind of hot. Yeah, okay let's go see if he has that one new song.

TRICIA: What new song?

STACEY: You know that one. The one I like.

TRICIA: Which one is that?

STACEY: You know the one that goes like this … (*she tries to hum the song*)

TRICIA: Oh, yeah, he's going to know that one right off… (*rolls her eyes*) You don't even know the name of the song.

JENNIFER: Don't worry, I'm sure he'll have it.

(*JENNIFER, TRICIA, and STACEY begin to leave when BEN ENTERS with PRINCESS TOLSKA.*)

JENNIFER: Go ahead, I'll be right there.

(TRICIA and STACEY EXIT.)

JENNIFER: Ben, where is your alien friend, Tootsie?

BEN: Tookie & Tonk are handing candy out at the door to the Trick or Treaters?

JENNIFER: What are you guys thinking, leaving them alone like that!

BEN: Ellen is with them.

JENNIFER: Ben!

BEN: Okay, excuse me. I'll be back.

JENNIFER: Hello, I'm sorry I don't know your name? I'm Jennifer. Do you go to my school?

PRINCESS TOLSKA: No, I'm here to see Tonk and Tookie.

JENNIFER: Tonk and Tookie? Um, how do you know them? (*getting mad*) Ben! He told you, didn't he? That little booger! He wasn't supposed to tell anyone. I could kill him.

PRINCESS TOLSKA: No, he doesn't know me either. I'm from a planet named Tish-ka-la-man-ta. I am the international greeter to all aliens visiting earth. Tonk and Tookie are on Rama, and their time is nearly up, and they must return home.

JENNIFER: What's Rama?

PRINCESS TOLSKA: Rama is a Marshian rite of passage. After they return and report their findings to the hierarchy. If they have done well.

Then they will be assigned to positions of talent among their people.
JENNIFER: So this is pretty important stuff for them.
PRINCESS TOLSKA: You could say that.
JENNIFER: I thought I had that one wrapped up. I've been pretty annoyed that they showed up here! Tonight of all nights. I didn't even consider that maybe their being here was important to them.
PRINCESS TOLSKA: It's a very human way of thinking.
JENNIFER: Well, I hope they had a blast and that they will remember this night forever. I know I will never forget it.
(ELLEN, BEN, TONK, and TOOKIE ENTERS.)
TONK and TOOKIE: Princess Tolska, your honor. (they do an alien greeting) Our pleasure is found in your keeping!
PRINCESS TOLSKA: Tonk and Tookie, it is time to return to Marsha and end your Rama.
TONK: Thank you, Ellen, and Ben. We have had much pleasure here on Earth. Many things about tonight will be reported and will please the ears of my people. Especially about candy! May I take candy home with me?
BEN: You may have as much as you'd like.
TOOKIE: I will teach Marshians about dancing and Hip Hop. I have downloaded all three hundred and forty-two songs into my memory.
ELLEN: It has been an amazing experience.

JENNIFER: I just wanted to say I'm sorry that I such an unwelcoming hostess tonight.
TONK: Ellen said you wanted to be a cheerleader.
TONK & TOOKIE: Hip hip hooray. (they do an Alien kind of cheer)
   (JENNIFER, ELLEN, AND BEN laugh.)
PRINCESS TOLSKA: Tonk, Tookie it is time.
TONK & TOOKIE: Goodbye, earthlings.
BEN, JENNIFER, and ELLEN: Goodbye.
(TONK, TOOKIE, and PRINCESS TOLSKA EXIT the kitchen door. While BEN JENNIFER and ELLEN watch from the window.)
JENNIFER: Sorry guys for being so bossy. Ben if you want to go tell Mom and Dad, you can.
BEN: No, don't worry about it. They'd never believe me. But I will let you explain to Dad how his antique clock got taken apart by Tonk.
JENNIFER: Seriously! Ben, I'm going to kill you! How could you let that happen?
ELLEN: Breathe, Jennifer. Just breathe.

THE END

More Plays like this can be found in our 10 Minute Play Series

Available for purchase on Amazon.com

Made in the USA
Columbia, SC
17 April 2025